Music
Through
the Floor

STORIES

ERIC PUCHNER

SCRIBNER
New York London Toronto Sydney

7
Puchner

SCRIBNER
1230 Avenue of the Americas
New York, NY 10020

SCRIBNER and design are trademarks of
Macmillan Library Reference USA, Inc., used under license
by Simon & Schuster, the publisher of this work.

For information about special discounts for bulk purchases,
please contact Simon & Schuster Special Sales:
1-800-456-6798 or business@simonandschuster.com

Designed by Kyoko Watanabe
Text set in Sabon

Manufactured in the United States of America

1   3   5   7   9   10   8   6   4   2

Library of Congress Cataloging-in-Publication Data
Puchner, Eric.
Music through the floor : stories / Eric Puchner.
p. cm.
Contents: Children of God—Essay #3 : Leda and the swan—Child's Play—
Diablo—Neon tetra—Legends—A fear of invisible tribes—
Animal here below—Mission.
PS3616.U25M87 2005
813'.6—dc22   2005049972

ISBN-13: 978-0-7432-7046-5
ISBN-10: 0-7432-7046-0

Versions of these stories have previously appeared elsewhere:
"Children of God" in *Zoetrope: All-Story* and *Pushcart Prize: Best of the Small
Presses 2004*; "Essay #3: Leda and the Swan" in *Epoch* and *Best New American
Voices 2005*; "Child's Play" in *Boulevard*; "Diablo" in *The Missouri Review*;
"Neon Tetra" in *Glimmer Train*; "Legends" in *Cimarron Review*;
"Animals Here Below" in *Zoetrope: All-Story*; and "Mission" in *Chicago Tribune*.

For Katharine,
and in memory of my father

Contents

Music
Through
the Floor

Children of God

THE AD SAID THEY NEEDED SOME-
one to model "patterns of survival." At the
interview, a woman with an *E.T.* poster on her door told me
about the job. "You'd be working at their house," she said,
"taking care of two clients with special needs."

I couldn't even take care of myself, but I needed a job. "Are
they retarded?"

"Okay, yeah. We don't say that anymore." She coaxed herself out of a frown, in a way that suggested I was the only candidate. "There's a new name: developmentally disabled."

They gave me a new name, too: Community Living Instructor. This was in Portland, Oregon. I started working at a home
for people who couldn't tie their shoes, helping two grown men
get through the day.

• • •

Jason was worse off. At twenty-eight, he was afflicted with so many diseases that his meds were delivered in a garbage bag. He made Job look like a whiner. Enlarged by hydrocephalus, his head drooped from his body, which twisted in his wheelchair as if it were trying to unscrew from his neck. His mouth hung open in a constant drool. His hands, crippled from dystrophy, curled inward as though he wanted to clutch his own wrists. Among other things, he was prone to seizures and cataleptic fits. He had chronic diarrhea. Every evening, after dinner, I was met with a smell so astounding I had to plug my nose with cotton. I'd wheel Jason, besmirched and grinning, to the bedroom to change his mess. "I made a bad, bad meeeesss!" he'd yell, flapping his arms. "Now we're cooking with oil!" For the most part, his vocabulary consisted of clichés he'd picked up from former care workers, many of them bizarre or unsavory to start with: "cooking with oil" was one, as was "you said a mouthful when you said that." Other times, he was capable of surprising clarity. He loved action movies—particularly ones in which nature avenged itself on humanity—and would recount the death of a dinosaur hunter as if it were a sidesplitting joke.

The changing of the mess, though, was the high point of Jason's day. He giggled uproariously when I lifted him from the wheelchair, his arms kinked around my neck as I carried him to bed. He never failed, during our brief walk together, to burrow his tongue deep into my ear.

Dominic was more serious. Brooding, treacherously off balance, he staggered around the house like a drunk. Down syndrome had smudged his face into the flat, puttylike features of a Hollywood gangster. He was beautiful in a way that startled women. He was thirty-two years old and owned a bike with a banana seat and training wheels. The bike was supposed to be impossible to tip over. He'd strap a helmet on his head and wiggle into an armature of pads and then go for a ride down the street, returning ten minutes later covered in blood. I cleaned his wounds with a sponge. About ten times a day, he'd sneak into the bathroom to "fresh his breath." He always left the door open, and I'd watch him sometimes from the hall. He'd nurse the faucet first, sucking on it until his mouth filled with water. Then he'd pop up suddenly and arch his back in a triumphant stance, face lifted toward the ceiling. Sometimes he'd stay like that for thirty seconds—moaning, arms outstretched, eyes shut tight like a shaman receiving prophecies—before puking his guts out in the sink.

His voice, when he spoke, was sleepy and far-fetched. He preferred the middles of words. "Abyoola!" he liked to say, meaning "Fabulous!" When he told a story, it was like Rocky Balboa channeling a demon.

I'd moved to Portland after a month of sleeping in my car, driving aimlessly around the West and living off my father's Mobil card. The driving had to do with a frantic feeling in my stomach. I felt like Wile E. Coyote when he goes off a cliff, stranded in midair and trying to crawl back to the edge before he plummets. In the glove box, sealed with plastic and a rubber band, was a Dixie cup of my mother's ashes that I'd nabbed from her memorial when I was twelve. I kept it there for good luck. Before my month of driving, I'd taped Sheetrock in Idaho, sold vacuum cleaners in Missoula, Montana, worked as a baggage handler at the Salt Lake City airport.

To pass the day, I took Jason and Dominic on field trips. There was a special van in the garage, and I'd load Jason onto the lift and strap down his wheels so he wouldn't roll out the window. The van had been donated by a traveling magician and was painted purple. We'd drive to cafés, outdoor fairs, movie theaters. They liked easy-listening stations—"I Write the Songs," "Send in the Clowns"—and I'd crank the old AM stereo as loud as it would go. I'd roll down the windows and listen to Jason scream words at the top of his lungs, naming the passing creatures of the world like Adam on a roller coaster. "Dog!" he'd yell. "Girl! Pizza boy!" Dominic would stick his head out the window of the front seat, his hair exploding in the wind. Someone had taught him how to flip people off and he'd give pedestrians the finger as we passed. It was a good test of character, and I liked watching people question the simplicity of innocence.

Once, at a stoplight, a guy in a fraternity sweatshirt returned the gesture and then strode up to Dominic's side of the van, his girlfriend sloping behind him. The guy's arm was outstretched to better advertise his finger, which he was following like a carrot.

"What the fuck, man," the guy said to Dominic. "You looking for a new asshole?"

Dominic wagged his finger at the guy's face, enjoying himself immensely. "We're going to get some ice cream," I explained.

The guy took a closer look at Dominic and turned red. He dropped his hand and glanced at his girlfriend, who was regarding him with distaste.

"You should teach them some manners," he mumbled. "This isn't the goddamn circus."

At Baskin-Robbins, we waited in line while the customers ahead of us sucked on little spoons. Dominic ogled the women. He was a pervert only because of his IQ; otherwise, he'd have been concealing his interest like the rest of us. It was more metaphysical than sexual. Sometimes I'd find him staring at a lingerie-clad model in a magazine, struck dumb with fervor, his lips moving silently as if in prayer.

While we waited, Jason slumped in his wheelchair and I wiped the drool from his chin. The woman in front of us kept glancing back at him. It was always the same expression, a coded kind of smile directed at me as well, like we shared some secret knowledge about the afterlife.

Finally, she couldn't resist any longer and squatted beside Jason. "What's your favorite flavor?" she brayed, as if she were speaking to a foreigner.

He seemed to study the case of ice cream. "Like trying to sell Jesus a jogging suit!"

"That's right, dear," the woman muttered but didn't talk to him again.

When it was Dominic's turn to order, he staggered around the counter before I could stop him and stood by the cash register. The girl behind the counter laughed. He stared at her breasts without speaking. I might have done something to ward off disaster, but I wanted to see what would happen.

"Show me what you want," she said. It was the wrong thing to say. Dominic grabbed one of her breasts. "Hey," the girl said, laughing. She tried to pull away and he held on, clutching at her shirt. He wore an expression of deep, incredulous despair. "Hey!" the girl said. Finally, I ran around the counter and pulled Dominic off with two hands, leading him back to the customer side, where he seemed unembarrassed by his conduct.

It was always like that: the world scorned them, but they were freely and openly themselves. I admired them greatly. We tried to order ice cream, but the girl was shaken and refused to serve us.

I lived in a studio apartment with no phone. The only piece of furniture was a pea-colored sofa I'd bought at the Goodwill and dragged up five flights of stairs by myself. For three days, because of my poor grasp of geometry, it remained lodged vertically in the doorway. I was still on the Mobil dining plan: maple bars and hot dogs and Snapple iced tea. I had a box of books and a box of cooking utensils, but I never unpacked them.

My dad moved away when I was in college and took up with an ex–movie star. Actually, she wasn't a movie star at all but somebody who used to stand in for movie stars during long or onerous rehearsals. She hadn't been on a set for years but liked to talk about "Bob" Redford and "Marty" Sheen. My father had convinced her he was rich. Now they lived in Utah, in the middle of the desert, and he was taking care of her children.

I'd called my dad from a pay phone, the month I was living out of my Subaru.

"You surprised me," he said. "Where are you?"

"Las Vegas."

"Jesus, Drew. What are you doing in Vegas?"

"Good one. Seeing some friends." Actually, I'd spent the afternoon in a casino bathroom, shivering on the toilet and battling suicidal fantasies, visions of myself with my brains blown out and soaking in a puddle. "I was thinking I'd drive up and stay with you guys for a few days."

"Sure," he said. "That would be fine. I mean great. Come on up." He hesitated, and I could hear a woman's voice in the background. "It's Drew," my dad said. "Drew? Hang on a sec, will you?"

He put his hand over the receiver. For a long time, I couldn't hear anything but the ring of a slot machine behind me. Then the sound came back and I caught the tail end of a sentence in the background, the woman's voice saying, "running a B & B."

"Drew? This weekend's a little hectic. You know we've got five of us here already and the place is a mess."

I laughed, but it sounded as far off as the slot machine. *Chink chink chink.*

"The thing is," my dad said, "I'm not sure where you'll sleep."

"Jackpot," I said before hanging up. "Do you hear that?"

Every afternoon, at Jason and Dominic's, we'd sit at the dining room table and sift through the day's mail, giggling at the letters addressed to "Cigar Lover" or "Channel Surfer." Sometimes, from the mailbox on the corner, I'd send them postcards I'd collected on my travels, thirty-cent souvenirs picturing places like Orchard Homes, Montana, or Mexican Hat, Utah. "Wish you were here!" I'd write. Or "Having the time of my life!" We put the postcards in a shoe box in case the happy stranger returned.

One day, sometime in March, Dominic got a sweepstakes letter and we opened it excitedly. I filled out the necessary information, showing him how to paste the publisher's stamps in the little squares. For a week after we'd sent it in, he seemed mercurial, distracted. He was particularly excited about the grand prize—a 1969 Mustang convertible with a galloping horse on the grille—and I helped him put the glossy picture of it on the refrigerator.

Filling in for a graveyard shift one night, I started from a nap at 5:00 a.m. when the front door creaked open. I went to investigate and saw Dominic sitting on the steps like a gloomy wino in his Fruit of the Looms, squinting at the half-lit street.

"What are you doing, Dominic?" I asked, putting my hand on his shoulder.

"Ooing," he said, in his no-consonant drone.

"Yes, doing. It's five in the morning."

He looked at me queerly. "Ar," he said, meaning "car." Since his subjects were limited, I'd learned to translate his words into their probable correlates. "Red car no roof!" he explained.

In my tired state, I pictured the red convertible rolling down the street, tied up with a giant bow. I explained to him the chances were one in a trillion. "There's no car, Dominic. It's a scam—a game, you see? We just did it for fun. You've got no chance at all."

He stared at me without comprehending. "Car! Red car go fast!"

"Besides, you can't drive. You'd crash it anyway."

"No crash!" he said angrily, rising to his feet.

Spit flew from his lips. Such passion! I would have given anything to care like that. I got Dominic to bed finally but lay wide-eyed on the couch, relapsing into suicidal fantasies. *Live each day as your last,* they say, but nobody in their right mind would try it. I reminded myself that it was Jason's birthday tomorrow, that I was the only one—of the three of us—who knew how to bake a cake.

The next afternoon I returned to the house and started getting ready for the party. We strung up balloons, and I bought party hats and noisemakers. Jason's parents were supposed to arrive at three o'clock. At 2:45, the phone rang and a woman's voice drawled bashfully into my ear. She told me that their car was in the shop with brake trouble.

"I'm so sorry. I know Jason was expecting us."

"He's waiting for his presents," I said.

She fumbled with the phone. "I can't tell you. We feel just awful about this."

"Look, we'll just come over there. Give me your address. I'll bring the cake and noisemakers."

An awkward pause. "Oh, no. Don't trouble yourself. I mean, it's too far a drive for them. They won't enjoy it."

"It's no trouble," I said loudly. "They love riding in the van."

It was a long ride on the freeway and we heard "Send in the Clowns" two times. Jason sat in the back, displaying none of his customary excitement at being on the road. "It's your birthday," I kept reminding him. When I told him we were going to see his parents, he just stared out the window with his head wilting like a sunflower. Eventually we found the exit and climbed a steep suburban street into some hills, rising above the great cloverleaf of the freeway into a development of newly built houses. I looked for some signs of recognition on Jason's face, but then realized he may never have been there before.

Jason's parents greeted us at the door and invited us into the kitchen. Even though it was rainy season, they both had sunburns. Their faces were blank behind their smiles: I could have shaken them like an Etch A Sketch and made them disappear. The Kreighbaums seemed shy around their son, talking to him in special voices and exchanging covert looks. Mr. Kreighbaum wore a winded expression that emphasized the redness of his face, as if he'd just completed a succession of cartwheels. He watched me empty the contents of the bag I'd brought, peering at the party favors I laid out on the counter.

The whole place made my teeth hurt. In fact, I was clenching them in rage.

"Put on a party hat," I commanded Mr. Kreighbaum.

"Oh, no." He chuckled, glancing at his wife. "I don't think it'll fit."

"I promised Jason."

He took the little hat from my hand, sneaking a glimpse out the window before stretching the elastic cord around his chin. His head looked gigantic under the paper cone of the hat. We walked, wheeled, and staggered into the dining room and sat at the long oak table, which held a meager stack of presents. Mrs. Kreighbaum brought out plates of fruit salad and served us without speaking. I went to the kitchen and reentered with the cake, and we sang "Happy Birthday" to Jason, but he just sat there and refused to blow out his candles. His eyes were rheumy and distracted. I tried to cheer him up with a noisemaker, but he batted it from his face with one hook.

"When's the last time you've seen Jason?" I asked Mrs. Kreighbaum.

She looked at her husband. "I don't know. Gosh." She turned her smile in my direction. "He seems so happy where he is."

"I'm gonna open up a can of whup-ass," Jason said.

Mr. Kreighbaum tried to interest him in the presents, but he pushed them away with a listless shove. Undeterred, Mr. Kreighbaum opened up the biggest box on the table, feigning surprise at the contents. It was a plastic trout that flapped its tail when you came near it and sang "Take Me to the River." You were supposed to hang it on the wall. Clearly, the resourceful man had run out to Walgreens before we got there and bought whatever he could find.

He slid the toy from its box and laid it on the table to demonstrate. The trout was more convincing as an allegory of death, flapping its tail against the table and pleading for our mercy. Jason, incredibly, showed little interest. In the end Mr. Kreighbaum had to open the presents himself, slumped over the table in his party hat, holding each toy up for our approval.

Mrs. Kreighbaum—out of politeness, probably—tried to engage Dominic. "How's the fruit salad?" she asked.

"Abyoola!"

"Amen on that," I said to Dominic. "I agree with you one hundred percent."

Dominic asked where the bathroom was, and I had to repeat the question before Mrs. Kreighbaum would answer him. He lurched out of his chair. I thought he might knock something over, but he fumbled his way down the hall without disaster. Soon we could hear the *yaak*s and spits, the sounds of exultant retching.

"It's a masturbation thing," I explained, trying to hide my elation. "He's sexually frustrated."

About halfway through the presents, Jason got a sheepish, self-occupied look. The stench was tremendous. It was no illusion: we were working together. I let the Kreighbaums sit there for a while, watching them stare at their plates while the house echoed with bulimic groans.

"Do you have any diapers?" I asked eventually.

Mrs. Kreighbaum shook her head. I went to get an Attends from the emergency stash in the van and threw the diaper in Mr. Kreighbaum's lap. I asked him to change Jason in the bedroom, managing to bestow the task with a sense of honor. He glanced at his wife—a quick, despondent peek—and then looked at me pitifully.

"I think Susie might be better equipped."

"He only lets men," I said.

"But I'm his mother!" Mrs. Kreighbaum said.

"Please—this is no time to take things personally." I turned to Mr. Kreighbaum. "Grab a bucket and some dish towels. You'll need to wipe him down first."

He nodded. Clutching the Attends like a book, Mr. Kreighbaum stood up obediently and rummaged under the sink in the kitchen until he found an empty paint can. He held it up for approval and then wheeled Jason through the open doorway at the far end of the hall. The door closed behind them with an air of doom. Mrs. Kreighbaum and I picked at the remnants of our cake. Something about her face, the way it stared helplessly into her plate, gave me a twinge of guilt.

Eventually the noises stopped and Dominic staggered back into the dining room, grinning from exhaustion, eyes glazed from the effort of his puking. He smiled at Mrs. Kreighbaum and said something I couldn't decipher. She glanced at the closed door at the end of the hall, eyeing it with a look of canine longing. How hard was it to change a diaper? I asked her to watch Dominic and then went down the hall to investigate.

It was worse than I'd expected. Jason, naked and white as a canvas, was curled up on the king-size bed, his ass and legs obscured by a painterly mess. Mr. Kreighbaum stood above him with sagging shoulders, hair thorned with sweat, holding a wet rag that was dripping on the carpet. The party hat had slipped down and was sticking out of the front of his forehead. He looked like a big, melanomic unicorn. There was shit on his hands and shirt and all over the denim comforter covering the bed. His hands trembled. He looked at me in despair, surrendering eagerly to defeat, like a refrigerator repairman asked to do an autopsy.

I burned the image in my mind, savoring it while I could.

I brushed Mr. Kreighbaum aside and cleaned Jason myself, changing his Attends and setting him carefully back in the wheelchair. He looked at his father and laughed out loud. "You're cruising for a bruising!" he said. He giggled all the way back to the dining room, his mood magically improved. Dominic, however, had disappeared.

"I asked you to watch him!" I said.

Mrs. Kreighbaum clutched a chair. "I had to use the restroom."

I saw that she was crying. My teeth had stopped hurting, finally, but I didn't feel any better. The two of us went to look for Dominic and found him standing by the curb across the street, bent over someone's Jetta and peering through the window like a burglar. The dandruff in his hair sparkled in the sun. He turned to us with yearning, half-open eyes.

"Red," he mumbled. "My car for zoom."

"That's not your car," I said. "We're at the wrong house completely."

* * *

On the way home, we stopped at Burger King for some Whoppers and sat next to an elderly woman with gigantic eyes filling her glasses. She watched Jason and Dominic maul their food, smiling in that special way when I caught her eye.

"Children of God," she whispered, leaning across her table and nodding seriously.

I couldn't suppress a laugh. Jason, who'd been observing the scene with an amused look, tugged at my elbow.

"What did she say?" he asked.

"She called you 'children of God.'"

He guffawed. "Children of Gaawwd?"

"That's right," I said, practically guffawing myself.

The lady turned white. Dominic soon picked up on the joke and joined us in our laughter, gasping out wild, choking horse-laughs, the three of us splitting our sides until we almost fell out of our seats.

Occasionally, after my shift with Jason and Dominic, I'd go to a bar on my street to get drunk. It was the kind of place with a neon martini glass for a name and an unsinkable turd floating in the toilet. Each time the same middle-age boat worker would buy me drinks. She cleaned yachts on the Willamette and her skin reeked of chemicals. Years in the sun had crumpled her face. She took classes at the hatha yoga center next door and was always waiting at the bar with her rolled-up mat, like a hobo.

When she got drunk, she'd stand on her head to prove she could drive. She was the only alcoholic yoga enthusiast I'd ever met. Once she asked me what I did for a living.

"I work with some retards," I said.

"Right," she said, commiserating. "I know what you mean."

After the fourth or fifth drink, I'd wait until she went to the bathroom before escaping out into the night.

• • •

In the mornings before work, I'd take long strolls through the industrial streets of Portland, muttering to myself in a somnolent daze. I walked the same streets every day but never knew where I was. The fog hung in shreds; I stepped through secret portals and found the sun. It was the fantasies—the suicide fog in my head—that I couldn't step out of. The fact that I was going crazy crossed my mind more than once, but the beauty of the city distracted me, the ivy-covered walls and elegantly trussed bridges. In stores, I found it difficult to talk to people: my mouth floundered out a Dominic-style vowelese that made cashiers pull back in disgust. I felt like a visitor from another planet, inhabiting some poor earthling's body.

"Are you all right?" someone asked when I was having trouble buying groceries. The little machine at the counter, and then the checkout girl herself, kept asking for my PIN number. I knew the PIN was my birth date, that wasn't the problem. The problem was I couldn't remember when I was born.

"Of course not," I said, losing patience. "You're being . . . rhetorical?"

The man stepped back. "I was trying to help."

"Look, you're driving me up the wall."

I would weep for no reason, sometimes for hours. A physical condition. My heart was an onion making me cry. I started arriving earlier and earlier at Jason and Dominic's, relieving other people before their shifts were done.

Once, driving back from the movies, we passed by a long, sprawling cemetery bristling with tombstones. Jason seemed very interested in the graves, even the ones without balloons tied to them. I watched his face grow shyly contemplative in the rearview mirror.

"Dead guys," I explained.

"Why?" he said, staring out the window.

"You mean why are they dead?" I was impressed by his curiosity. "Excellent question. Superb." I tried to think, a painful undertaking. "Maybe they were jealous of the dead people. I mean, when they were alive. They got tired of shitting themselves. You know, like an escape—except you go under the ground."

"Under the ground?" He was grinning, though he seemed confused. "So what do they eat?"

"They're just bones. They don't know how to eat."

I thought he might be alarmed by this, but he found it very amusing. "They don't know how to . . . eat?" he spat out, before convulsing with laughter.

Dominic picked up on the joke, and the two of them giggled, trading smirks. Of course it was funny—all those drastically stupid skeletons. When we got back, I walked them to my car and showed them the Dixie cup of ashes in the glove box, explaining how the gray silt used to be a person. I thought they should know their alternatives. Dominic, in particular, greeted the idea with scorn. "No clean!" he said. I handed the ashes to Jason, who thought they were meds and tried to lift them to his mouth.

The next day we went to a coffee shop on Hawthorne Boulevard and ran into the boat worker who liked to buy me drinks. She stared at us as we ordered three lattes with straws in them. In the daylight, sitting by herself in the corner, she looked less toxic. I introduced her to Jason and Dominic, who were impressed by her gender.

"Smell like blue!" Dominic said, sniffing her fingers.

"Cut it out," I told him.

"Blue water toilet!"

She looked at me, frowning. "These are your co-workers?"

"Best friends," I joked, pretending it wasn't true.

Dominic touched her hair. I'd forgotten her name and she told me, wincing a little.

"Mensa?" I said. "Like the whatever thing for geniuses?"

She shrugged. "My mom liked the sound of it."

I took her back to Jason and Dominic's, showed her the house where I spent most of my time. She burped for their entertainment and let Dominic hold her breast. We weren't used to having visitors and kept looking at ourselves in the mirror above the filing cabinet. After a little while, Mensa got up and started flipping through the cupboards in the kitchen.

"Don't they have anything to drink in this house?" she asked.

"I don't think that's one of their patterns of survival."

"Great. What about us?"

Later, we retreated to Jason's Flex-A-Bed while he and Dominic watched a video in the living room. Mensa's face was stitched with lines, like an Arctic explorer's. I held her tight and curled my legs into her stomach. Dinosaurs roared in the background. She tried to interest me in other things, which annoyed me: I wanted to be clutched. I'd heard about a machine, invented by an autistic person, that would clench you in a giant rubber hand for as long as you needed.

"You're the most miserable lover I've ever had," she said, probing her nostril with a finger. She picked her nose without embarrassment, as if she were enjoying a cigarette.

"So I hear."

"No. I mean, I thought *I* had problems."

She started coming over in the afternoons, showing up after work in her coveralls. She had a flask with a golf ball on it that she'd stolen from one of the yachts she worked on. We'd fold together in Jason's bed and clutch each other until my arm went numb. The sweat in her hair smelled like Drāno. I didn't deserve a morsel of grace, even a noxious one, but no one had bothered to let her know. Afterward, she'd do yoga on the front lawn in the mizzling rain, lying on her back and then lifting herself slowly into an arch, like a demolition shown in reverse. The poses had mysterious names: Downward Dog, Sun Salute. Once I found her lying on the grass in a random-looking sprawl, the palms of her hands turned up to the drizzle.

"The Corpse," she explained later. "Feels wonderful."

Two months after visiting his parents, Jason had a grand mal seizure. It happened on the morning shift, but I got there in time to catch the paramedics loading his exhausted body into the ambulance, to see the gaunt perplexity of his face. We had a special employee meeting, and the Care Services Coordinator warned us Jason could die on anyone's shift; he'd already lived past his projected life span. The house was lonely without him, and I wondered if his parents were visiting him in the hospital.

When he got back, Jason seemed wan and listless. I changed his mess like always, but he didn't giggle or stick his tongue in my ear. When I tried to teach him some new clichés, he just stared at me with a drifting face.

His mother started dropping by now and then, treating me like a servant now that she was in her son's house. She read picture books to Jason while I cooked Hamburger Helper or prepared his meds. She always left after thirty minutes, mid-book, when she'd appeased her guilt for hoping he would die. His father never came.

To cheer him up, I brought Mensa to the house. She burped at Jason—his favorite trick—but he just stared at her without laughing. Then he rolled his eyes to the wall, trapped in a dream. Dominic sat on the front steps as usual, staring resolutely down the street with his hands folded in his lap, like a millennialist awaiting the Rapture. He'd sit there for a million years, while the glaciers returned and sharks waddled from the ocean. I felt a breathless envy that made me sick.

"You think he'd give a shit that his roommate's dying," I said.

"Probably it doesn't mean anything to him," Mensa said. "Life and death."

I went outside and interrupted Dominic's vigil.

"Red car!" he said, jumping up. "Fastest car!"

"Dominic, will you shut up?" He was excited and tottering. I had to grip his shoulders to steady him. "There's no car coming."

"Red car go zoom!"

"Dominic, listen to me!"

"Fabulous car!"

"You're not going to win anything!" I said, shaking him. His head flopped back and forth. "Can't you get that through your thick skull?"

Jason never went back to his original self. He sat in the back of the van and saved himself for special occasions, shouting out the window only at particularly ludicrous sights, like a dog or a hippie. He lost his sense of schadenfreude during movies and stopped guffawing when someone was killed or eaten.

When we passed the cemetery now, he stared out the window and eyed it suspiciously.

"Dead people," he said. His mouth changed at the corners, but I couldn't tell if it was a smirk or a frown.

"Yep." I knew what was coming.

"They don't know how to eat."

"That's right," I said cheerfully. "They're too stupid."

"We're smarter than them," he whispered with his head bowed, like a wish.

• • •

Mensa and I found a cheap body shop on Burnside and took my Subaru in for a paint job. I'd saved enough—using my dad's Mobil card on daily necessities—to pay for it. When the car was finished, we drove to the house and parked it on the curb. I brought Dominic outside with a blindfold on, leading him down the steps and untying it before he fell on his head.

He stood there for a minute, rubbing his eyes. Except in the movies, I'd never seen anyone rub their eyes in astonishment— but he actually put his fists to his eyes and ground them into the sockets.

"Red car," he said finally. He was stock-still on the sidewalk, the only time I'd seen him stand in one place without swaying like a mast. "My car win!"

"There's no room in the garage," I told him. "I'll have to keep it for you."

We took him for a test drive, speeding into NOT A THROUGH ROADS and startling neighbors. Back at the house, Mensa and I escaped to the bedroom. Dominic's excitement had gone to my head; I tried my best to emulate him, to imagine what he'd do in my situation. We lay in bed and I touched her breast through her coveralls, breathing in her scent. I was trembling with nerves but managed to get her clothes off without too much struggle. Her body was smooth and white, a distant memory of her face. I was still clothed, luckily, when we heard someone pull up the driveway. The donors. I'd forgotten all about them. I looked at Mensa, who was lying next to me in her underthings.

"They're here to take a tour."

"Now?" she said. "You mean, like, immediately?"

"Stay here," I told her.

I shut her in the bedroom and went out to greet the donors,

who were dressed in business clothes and inspecting the front azalea beds. These were the people, the guilty rich, who gave the agency money. I introduced them to Jason, who told them they were treading on thin ice and went back to his movie depicting the end of the world. I gave them a quick tour of the house, careful to avoid the bedroom. Just as I was leading them outside, Dominic returned from a bike ride toasting his sweepstakes win, covered in scrapes and bruises.

"He's bleeding!" the man said to me.

"It's normal. He's a hemophiliac."

"You mean he can't stop? Shouldn't he go to the hospital?"

I laughed. "It's not that kind of hemophilia, thank God!"

Dominic smiled triumphantly from under his helmet. I clapped him on the back and the donors relaxed, touched by our camaraderie. The man wanted to see the backyard. I tried to distract him with a description of Jason's and Dominic's more inspirational qualities, but he insisted on visiting the garden where "the residents had planted tomatoes." Probably it was the benchmark by which he gauged whether his money was being well spent. I led them toward the backyard, but when I reached the lawn I turned around and saw them standing in the middle of the brick path, transfixed by something in the house. They were staring at Mensa through the sliding glass doors of the bedroom. She'd gotten dressed, at least, but was hunched there in the center of the room, her face frozen into a spectral frown.

"I thought there were only two," the man said.

"Moved in last week," I explained.

She stared at us through the glass. Then she started to skulk back and forth, pushing her lips out from her face so they touched her nose. She stopped and picked up one of her cowboy boots from the floor, gnawing on it like a steak.

"What's she doing?" the woman asked reverently, leaning in my ear.

"One of our sadder cases—doesn't leave the bedroom."

Later, when we'd completed the tour, they shook Jason's and Dominic's hands, and the three of us accompanied them to their car. They seemed touched. They took a Polaroid of us in front of the house—a "family photo," the man called it—and we watched in astonishment as our faces stained the picture.

"This is good work, son," the man said. "Your parents must be proud."

That was the first day of July. Spring wound down into Portland's nicest time of year. The clouds broke and the city revealed itself for the first time, the great river shining in the sun. The river stayed in your eyes when you looked somewhere else.

Mensa spent long hours on the lawn, transforming herself into beautiful shapes. It was like an ancient kind of alphabet. Jason, Dominic, and I crowded near the window, wondering what she was writing. We watched her rise on her forearms and swing her body over her head in the form of a scorpion.

One day, she asked me outside to join her. I took off my shoes and followed her onto the lawn, feeling the warmth of grass between my toes. She taught me poses, whichever occurred to her at the moment: the Warrior, the Cobra, the Up-Facing Dog. As I warped my body into shapes, I had the sensation of leaving a message for someone I couldn't see. Mensa and I sprawled on the grass and closed our eyes without moving—for what seemed like forever. Then we stood up and she showed me how to salute the sun.

Later, we decided to take the red-painted Subaru out for a spin. I told Dominic that I had to do the driving, at least until he got a license, but that he could help me steer if he wanted. Jason lay across the backseat, his head propped on Mensa's lap. She stroked his hair and named what we passed. "Fire hydrant," she said. "Anarchists." I started out slowly but then picked up speed on the highway, cranking the easy-listening station as loud as it would go. It was like old times. I let Dominic have the wheel and he honked at two women in a Jeep, sure of his irresistible allure.

We drove out to the country, where the radio went static. The cows moped around like ghosts. When we stopped the car to say hello, they tried to memorize our faces.

On the way back, a gust rose from the fields and an old sign lifted out of the bed of a dump truck in front of us, held aloft by the wind. It sailed toward us in slow motion, levitating over the highway. FREE DELIVERY, it said. I almost shut my eyes. Instead, I veered out of the way and lost control of the wheel. We rocked into a ditch on the side of the road, the glove box flying open in a puff of gray powder. The four of us bounced in our seats. A second wind whipped through the Subaru and vanished into silence.

Our faces were dusted with ash. "Crazy idiot!" Mensa said—to the dump truck, I suppose.

"We're alive," I said. "That's what's important."

"Alive?" Jason asked.

We stared at each other, hearts pounding, and then I started the car again and headed for home.

Essay #3:
Leda and the Swan

A LTHOUGH THE SWAN IS NOT A delicate creature like a butterfly, and is not cuddly and cute like a kitten, it is a living thing that can feel pain and hunger just like any other living creature. In "Leda and the Swan," by William Butler Yeats, a perverted sort of swan ends up performing sexual intercourse with a loose girl named Leda. The motive of the swan is shown when he performs only a few foreplays, like caressing her "thighs" and gripping her "helpless breast," before revealing his "feathered glory."[1] He's got only one thing on his mind: shuddering his loins. This swan is clearly a sex-starved animal that doesn't

---

[1] William Butler Yeats, *Selected Poems and Three Plays* (New York: Macmillan, 1986), lines 2–6.

belong in Ireland, let alone a city park! In this essay, I will argue that Mr. Yeats is actually a mentally ill person who lives poetically through swans and furthermore knows nothing about swans and their gentile mating habits.

First of all, Mr. Yeats is a mentally ill person who lives poetically through swans. I know this for a fact because my older sister, Jeanie, is mentally ill and used to write poems about animals before she ran away from home to become a missing person. However, since she isn't a pervert, the poems were not about intercoursing swans. Instead, they were about animals we see on our tables every day. One of the poems (which I still have) goes like this:

> Cow, what do you chew?
> Big peace, bothering no one
> Who later chews you.[2]

This is not an American poem, because it has syllables. In fact, it is a haiku, which is a popular form of expression in Japan. Jeanie wrote this after I stole her boyfriend and she started to become mentally ill. Mentally ill people come in many different guises, and for Jeanie the guise was Veganism, a religion where you can't eat eggs or dairy products, such as cows. Like many poets, she has a soul that she wants to communicate with others and liked to put her poems on the refrigerator for everyone to read. Unfortunately, my stepfather Franz does not have the soul of a poet, especially if we're having stroganoff for dinner. Franz would often get angry and make many remarks about cows being more stupid than chickens. Franz grew up on a farm in Bavaria and knows a lot about the stupidity of

---

[2] Jeanie Mudbrook, "Cow Song," lines 1–3.

animals. One poem, in particular, seemed to upset him very much:

> *Turkey, my cousin*
> *We fail to be beautiful*
> *Punishment: oven.*[3]

Franz was upset because he felt like Thanksgiving dinner wasn't the best time for the reading of poetry, especially when he was eating a wing belonging to the protagonist of the poem. He said that Jeanie and the turkey must really be related if she would ruin a family get-together by reading a poem about the stupidest animal on Earth. Franz said that turkeys were so stupid you couldn't leave them out in the rain or else they'd drown. In fact, his family had lost a perfectly good turkey in Bavaria because his father had left it out in a thunderstorm by accident. Jeanie asked him if we should kill retarded people too because they're less intelligent than us, and Franz said no, we should leave them out in the rain first and see what happens. This made me laugh, but Jeanie didn't think it was very funny. She called him a Nazi. This was very bad, and mentally ill, because Franz is not a Nazi even though he thinks Germany's the best country in the world.

Actually, Jeanie was upset because I'd invited Colin, her exboyfriend, to dinner. I didn't feel too bad because they'd only dated for two months before Colin dumped her, and surely Jeanie should have seen the perfect destiny of our match. Later Colin told me the truth, which was that he'd only gotten to know Jeanie in the first place because he was in love with me on account of my facial beauty. I can tell you right now that my

---

[3] Mudbrook, "Ugliness," lines 1–3.

sister's not so facially victorious. She's got our dad's nose, which is a shame because my mom's been married three times since my dad and all of our stepfathers have had noses that didn't say from across the street hello I'm a nose.

Anyway, Colin's dumping her for my less visible features may have had something to do with Jeanie's mental collapse. Poets are very unstable people who often go crazy or die, and I should say that Colin is very handsome and popular and we were all surprised when he decided to date Jeanie in the first place. He is in a band called Salacious Universe and has long hair and these perfect gold arms like when you put honey on toast (except there aren't usually hairs in your toast). He is a construction worker on the weekends and looking at his arms kind of makes me wiggle my toes in an unvolunteering way until my sandals fall off. The wiggling was inaugurated at my first Salacious Universe concert. As it turned out, Jeanie couldn't go to the concert because she was attending a Vegan rally in front of the Safeway near our house. The concert was in the school auditorium (maybe you remember, Mr. Patterson, the flyers with Colin's hands shooting thunderbolts?), and I went with my friends Tamara and Tamara. It's a little weird how they have the same name, but neither of them wants to be called Tammy or Tams or Mara or any nickname I can think of because that would mean the other one got to keep their real name and she didn't.

So we were waiting for Salacious Universe to come out, sitting in the front row actually, when Colin pranced onto the stage like a two-legged deer and picked up this guitar he has with a bumper sticker on it that says FEAR ME, BRETHREN. It was very hot in the auditorium, and I could smell the aroma of many armpits rafting in my direction. After the cheering died down, Colin started singing and his face kind of went fierce and angry and these very sexy wrinkles formed between his eyebrows. I said Tamara and she said what and I said no, *Tamara,* and *she* said what and I said isn't he the most incredible human being of the male persuasion on planet Earth and she said yeah I don't know what he sees in Jeanie the haikuist freak. Salacious Universe plays speed metal music, which if you don't know is very difficult and requires you to change fingers all the time. They started right away to perform masterpieces and I knew immediately that I was destined to live my life with Colin Sweep, lead singer of Salacious Universe. The only problem was Jeanie, but I tried not to be a victim of negative thinking and dwell on the fact that she was dating my destiny. Colin is an idiot savant, which means he could play music with better lyrics than William Butler Yeats even though he was failing trigonometry, chemistry, American history, Spanish, and (far as I know) this class as well. In any case, Colin had us all riveted to his lips as he sang the chorus to one of his tour de forces:

> *All you mortals, I can and will bend*
> *Cuz I'm the father of gods and men!*[4]

Believe me, everyone was screaming and wanting to intercourse him if they were either female or homosexual.

Then something happened that wasn't in the program. Right when Colin was achieving the height of his genius, there was a blackout and everything went dark. You could hear the band playing in the dark, but the electricity was gone and it was just a ghost-sound and not the real thing, like when you're talking to your stepgrandparents in Germany and your voice comes back to you all small and distant on the phone. Then the lights went on again and Colin was shocked. I mean "shocked" in the

---

[4]Colin Sweep, "Pagan Liver," 2004.

electrical sense, because the microphone made a weird zapping sound and Colin's hair stood up into a punk-rock hairstyle and he flew across the stage like a migrant bird. Everyone was concerned about his general health, including me, and I ran up onstage to give him mouth-to-mouth. By the time I got there, though, he'd already half-recovered and was blinking into space with a very sedated expression that said I'm having a one-on-one interview with the light.

That's how we ended up backstage, me and Tamara and Tamara. We were delighted to be official Salacious Universe groupies, even though I was clearly the main one and they were really just groupies of me. It was cooler behind the stage and I furthered the recovery of Colin's head by resting it against a papier-mâché stump. He knew who I was, of course, but I had to introduce him to the Tamaras since they were persistent in their appearance. He found it supremely cool that they had the same name, and Tamara and Tamara were both sort of non-plucked because they did not secretly believe it was cool at all. Tamara asked him why the song was called "Pagan Liver" since it had nothing to do with body parts, and he explained that it wasn't supposed to be a part of the body at all but a person who lives, like you're a Pagan and you live that way.

After packing up his stuff, Colin asked me if I wanted to walk with him to the pay phone on the other side of campus. (I didn't offer my cell phone, because I'd never walked even a few feet with a famous guitarist.) The stars were shining like distant balls of gas, and you could see the janitors sitting on the roof of the library, sharing a cigarette. It was all very peaceful and beautiful with the janitors talking in Spanish and the imported words floating on top of our heads. Everything was really quiet except for the inside of Colin's pocket, which jingled with coins on account of his pinball-playing habit. That was when he told me that he liked the way I looked. His hair was still sticking magically from his head, all bright and glowing, like each hair was partaking in photosynthesis from the moon. He said he was going to call Jeanie and tell her he couldn't take her to Hailu's Tofu Palace because something had come up, something unexpected, without telling her of course it was a secret crush on my face.

But then something truly unexpected happened. When he tried to put a quarter in the pay phone, it refused to part from his finger. He shook his hand, but the quarter just remained there, magnetically attracted to his skin. Colin looked kind of worried and then stuck his hand in his pocket again and pulled it out and there were quarters stuck to each of his fingers, like a mini-family of George Washingtons with very long necks. Of course, it scared me a little that his fingers could behave so strangely. After a minute, Colin's face sort of changed, and he got this weird grin and wiggled his fingers and they glittered in the moonlight. He touched one of the coin-fingers to my mouth, which caused a tiny spark to enter my lips and electrocute the butterflies in my stomach. I have to admit, it was spooky and frightening and very breathtaking but also the most exciting thing that has happened in my life up till now.[5]

So that was how I ended up stealing Jeanie's boyfriend. I know it isn't cool to steal other people's boyfriends, especially if those people are your flesh-and-bones sister, and as a general rule I try to avoid it—but this was destiny and you only get one chance to fill it or else it flaps away into the starry universe.

---

[5] Mr. Patterson, I know this is supposed to be a paper about literature, and the particular literature named "Leda and the Swan," but you also said that we could use examples from our own life if we found something of "universal interest." That's why I've departed on a tangent and am writing this essay about love. I guarantee, universally, if you asked people which they'd prefer—a topic about LOVE or one about PERVERTED SWANS—they'd choose mine in a second.

When I got home from the concert, I found Jeanie waiting on the porch in her favorite skirt and leather-free high heels. I realized that Colin had forgotten to call her on account of his fingers being so talented. Because I'm a very honest person, I told her in a considerate way that Colin had fallen in love with me, that he was very sorry for the misunderstanding about dating her to begin with. Jeanie just stared at me with this little smirk on her face, like she was experiencing some gas in her stomach. Jeanie's got these very smirkable bee-stung lips that kind of complement the humongous bee that must have stung her nose. She had an unburning cigarette in her hand and she started to tear off little pieces from the end of it, sprinkling the pieces on the porch like she was trying to grow a tobacco tree. (Even though she's a Vegan, she smokes about five hundred cigarettes in her bathroom every day, which seems a little contradicting to her cause.) This was about when I started to appreciate her mental illness. I mean, if you're mentally all right, and you've just found out that your boyfriend's dumped you for your sister, possibly because you're nasally obese, then wouldn't you be a little upset? An hour later, when I went downstairs to get some water before bed, I looked through the window and saw Jeanie sitting out there in the exact same place as before, hunched there in her skirt, even though Franz said it was cold enough to freeze the testicles off a brass monkey.

Jeanie didn't speak to me at all until Thanksgiving, when I invited Colin to the house and she read her Vegan haiku out loud before taping it to the refrigerator. To be honest, I was very hesitant to invite Colin at all, not only on account of Jeanie but because my mom is not a very gifted cook and likes to serve Bavarian carp salad as a tribute to Franz's ancestors. After Jeanie called him a Nazi, we were all sitting there very much alarmed because she stomped around the room and said "Hi Hitler!" until our plates shook and the saltshaker tipped over on the table. I knew she was really directing her Nazi-bashing at me and Colin, even though she'd ignored both of us since the beginning of dinner. She was wearing a Salacious Universe T-shirt with no bra underneath and her hair was very oily and Jamaican-looking. Franz grabbed her by the arm and forced her to sit down, saying he'd have her delivered to a mental institution if she didn't stop mistaking his identity. Hitler was a very evil man, but my stepfather is just a bald person who owns a tire shop and likes to watch women's volleyball on Channel 39. My mom was incredibly pleasureless because she'd made Jeanie a special turkey-free dinner with Not Dogs and thought it would be nice to put some gravy on them, not thinking that gravy is made from the destruction of living creatures and their boiled necks. She finished her glass of white wine and started to get very sympathetic with the turkey's plight, apologizing to the neckless bird when Franz broke off a wing or a drumstick. We all kind of lost our appetites, even Franz, who just sat there silently chewing without looking at anyone.

Jeanie looked at me for the first time and then picked up a knife from the table and pointed it in my direction. Her face was very decomposed, and for a second I thought she might try to stab me. But then she turned to Colin and said that he was a slut who only cared about getting intercoursed and didn't he remember how she'd written all of his songs anyway and what was he going to do now, since he couldn't even spell "gargoyle"? What about moving to Hollywood and being speed metalists together, like they'd planned? She was kind of smirking and crying at the same time. It's true that they were friends before they'd started to date, but I didn't believe that she'd written any of his Salacious Universe masterpieces, even though he did look a little sad when she insulted his spelling. Obviously, Jeanie was just tortured with jealousy. I can't help it if I'm genet-

ically attractive and have perfect skin and hazel eyes.[6] Some-
times she reminds me of Othello in the book we read by
William Shakespeare, even though he was a mentally ill African-
American with no real reason to act that way.

The next day Colin took me to get a tattoo, my first ever,
which I designed myself because I wanted something totally original if I was going to beautify my ankle on a permanent basis. Of
course I didn't tell Jeanie, who avoided me the whole week, even
when she came downstairs one night to watch a sleep-inducing
documentary about the Animal Liberation Front. I couldn't help
noticing that she was boycotting brassieres as well as meat.
When the scab came off my ankle, though, I was so excited that
I forgot about Jeanie's green-eyed jealousy and actually stopped
her in the hall to show it to her. She lost her smirk for a second
and seemed genuinely very surprised. After a brief silence, we
had a conversation that I've tried to record here for prosperity:

JEANIE: You received a tattoo of a TV set?
ME: It is not a TV set. It's a cobra.
JEANIE: I know I'm a mentally ill person who suffers from
hallucinations, but it looks just like a TV.
ME: In reality, the cobra is coiled up in a basket. Like a
snake charmer's. That's its head.
JEANIE: Why the [intercourse] does it have antenna?
ME: Those are bolts of electricity. From its eyes.
JEANIE: Ha ha ha ha! (MENTALLY ILL LAUGHTER)

Obviously, this was all it took for me to reach a sad conclusion about Jeanie's mental future. To make things worse, she

---

[6] I'm sorry to keep stressing this, Mr. Patterson, but I also want to make
sure you know who I am since you always confuse me in class with Maria
Zellmer, who sits in the back corner and digs the earwax from her ears.

started to entertain nighttime visitors in her bedroom without anyone's permission. This was very sluttish and maybe could have been prevented by medication, which makes it even sadder. Since my mom and Franz are very leftist and allow us to have visitors whenever we like, and there's a staircase that basically leads right up to Jeanie's room from the back door, our slut prevention is not as implemented as it could be. Over the next few weeks, when I got up in the middle of the night to visit the restroom, I'd stop sometimes in the hall and hear sounds of nature coming through the door of Jeanie's room. These sounds of nature consisted of Jeanie and some boy intercoursing between the sheets. Or else, if they weren't intercoursing, I'd hear them talking in a private way that I couldn't hear. I knew she wasn't dating anyone at school, which means she was performing a major exhibition of her vagina. I must have heard her with six or seven partners. It's very sad, Mr. Patterson, but I didn't like imagining my sister and some stranger making a beast with two backs.[7]

A couple weeks after Thanksgiving, I asked Colin if Jeanie had ever been a slut with him, because frankly it was bothering my peace of mind quite a bit. We were sitting behind the Church, which was Colin's name for the big electric plant where we sometimes went to pet heavily in his Wagoneer. It did kind of look like a church, with its big voltage things sticking up like spires, but I felt like Colin meant it another way as well. Like there was something churchy about its relationship to his head. He looked at me all serious with his face shining in the lights from the electric plant and said he wasn't interested in intercoursing Jeanie, that he'd been waiting for her beautiful younger

---

[7] I know now this means intercourse, and not a camel like I wrote on my last paper, but I think that literature—and especially literature by William Shakespeare—should be less fascist in what it means.

sister to turn sixteen, which made me feel better to the third degree. Then he said he wanted to show me something special. I was in reality a little nervous because of his incredible manliness, and because his eyes were gleaming in a weird way from the sulfur lights, like those reflector things on the pedals of a bike, but then he looked down and started to undo the buttons of his shirt with one hand in a very sexy method.

I was very stunned by what I saw. Starting near Colin's Adam's apple, and getting longer with each button he undid, was a big scar dissecting his otherwise perfect breasts and going all the way down to his belly button. It looked like a little pink snake crawling down his chest. He told me that when he was eight years old he had become very sick and unable to breathe, and that the doctors had had to give him open-heart surgery and repair his heart. What they did is take one of his valves out and put in a new one, except the new one was bionic and made of metal. I put my head to his chest, because he told me to, and I heard the buzzing of the electric plant all around us but also a little sound under Colin's ribs, a secret ticking in his heart, like a watch when you put it up to your ear. It made me very sad and amazed. I asked him if he was still in any danger, but he told me that his new valve worked perfectly as long as he didn't go bungee jumping or scuba diving in some really great barrier reef. I closed my eyes and didn't see Colin the famous singer of Salacious Universe but Colin the sick boy who couldn't breathe, a little shivering boy thinking he might not live past age whichever, sitting by himself in the cafeteria or library or boys' locker room, and it made my insides melt into Natalie soup. That's when I said I thought I was in love with him. Colin looked at me very carefully, like he was deep in thought and maybe remembering the suffering of his childhood. Then he said that he didn't ordinarily do this, not after knowing me such a short time, but that he felt an "electroaffinity" between us and thought that we should finalize our love in the back of the car, especially since the Wagoneer had collapsible seats.

The truth is, I was a virgin and therefore the anti-Jeanie, but I didn't really want to admit it out loud. I didn't want to intercourse anyone who didn't love me in the biggest, most eternal way possible. I told Colin I wasn't ready to go all the way, and he kind of smile-frowned and said that he loved me, he just wanted to prove it to me—that's all it was, a way of proving his love—but I said it was extremely important to me and I needed time to think about it before yielding to his loins. I got home late that night because Mom wants to empower us with our own curfews and then stopped in front of Jeanie's door, listening for sounds of sexual abandonment. I knew Jeanie was a mentally ill slut, but I felt kind of bad because we used to be best friends when we were kids and now she was just a human sex appliance with no moral fibers. I remembered how we used to play orphanage every day and pretend to scrub the floors to please the evil housemother, two orphans with very miserable histories, but then we'd escape from the orphanage and find a tree to sleep under in the backyard and sneak back into the house like it was a rich person's mansion, filling pillowcases with whatever things we could steal, candlesticks and spaghetti tongs and big hunks of cheese. We'd sit under the tree and take each stolen thing out one at a time, saying oh how beautiful until we were close to tears.

I saw that Jeanie's light was on and knocked on the door and she opened it in an extra-small T-shirt, one of those slut-shirts that have numbers on them like football jerseys. She stood there smirking in that mental way, holding her stuffed hippopotamus under one arm like she was performing a touchdown. She asked me what I wanted and I told her I just wanted to see how she was, which was actually kind of true, though I also wanted to know if she could tell me anything about Colin's sexual résumé. She didn't invite me into her room so we stood there in the hall. I wanted to ask her if she remembered being kids, how we used to cry like stupid babies over spaghetti tongs, just to turn her mouth into something less smirky—but I didn't, of course. Instead I peered into her eyes and asked her if she loved the boys she intercoursed, except I used a less ethical word.

She seemed very unshocked and even laughed. Love's a joke, she said. Do you think Mom loves Franz? Do you think the President loves the First Lady? Do you think anybody loves anybody? I told her that love *had* to exist. Why else would people keep getting married all the time? Jeanie seemed to find this very smirk-inducing. Mom's been married four times—do you think she ended up loving any of them? How many of your friends' parents are still married? I didn't know what to say to that. It's true that almost all of them are divorced: Tamara's parents are divorced, and so are Tamara's, and actually I couldn't think of any original parents who seemed very much in love. And certainly Mom hasn't excelled in the romance category, seeing how we've had a new stepdad every four years—and now she and Franz's heads weren't exactly over their heels either, if you take into consideration that they yelled at each other every night about who should have put gas in the car or did she recycle the newspaper article about American children having lower IQ scores than Europe.

Still, I felt like I had to defend the most important part of my life, even if I had my own doubts about the future. I looked Jeanie in the eyeballs and told her that anyway *I* was in love, and that nothing else mattered. This actually did end Jeanie's smirk, because she looked at me kind of like she was the rich mother of the mansion pitying a starving girl orphan. She dropped her head a little bit and said that she needed to tell me something about Colin, that he'd never actually broken up with her completely. In fact, ever since Thanksgiving, he'd been visiting her room in the middle of the night while I was asleep! It wasn't just to relieve his loins either: they'd talk until morning sometimes, about the universe and its general lack of meaning and how they were the only people at school who knew that we were all just animals. He could never dump her for good, because their brains were conjoined. Jeanie was staring at Hippo and wouldn't meet my eye, and really I had to guess that she was speaking to me at all.

You don't even know what's real! I said.

I felt very depressed after our conversation, even though I knew Jeanie was extremely diluted and making up stories. I went downstairs to see if I could locate my mother. Instead I found Franz sitting in the TV room watching beach volleyball on Channel 39 and eating a carton of Häagen-Dazs vanilla fudge ice cream. He did what he always did when I discovered him watching women's volleyball, which was to get a blushing face and then tell me how he enjoyed the game of volleyball because of its "strategic nuance." I didn't see much strategic nuance, whatever that means, except that the players kept having to brush sand from their buttocks after they dove, which meant that there were four buttocks on each side to de-sand. I sat down with Franz to try to appreciate the game of volleyball, but when I asked him what the score was he said he wasn't sure.

So I went upstairs and knocked on my mother's door. As usual, she was drinking white wine because of her nerve-wrecking marriage and lying in bed with the covers pulled up to her waist. I asked her if she was all right, and she said that yes, of course she was all right, if you call being married to a Nazi tire salesman with one ball all right, then I should send my congratulations to Eva Braun. I had no idea what she was talking about, at least with the congratulations part, and I was worried that she might be getting mentally ill like my sister because I'd heard about these things running in the family. She asked me if I knew who else had one testicle, and I said no, and she said Hitler! I was very upset that Franz had the same testicles as Adolf Hitler, because I wasn't even aware that he was disabled. I wanted to make her feel better, so I crouched beside her and took her glass of wine away and then kind of tucked her into bed like she used to do when I was a girl. It's a weird thing, tucking in your own mother, and I don't really recommend it unless you're a professional nurse and have a diploma in drunk-mother-tucking. Before I turned off the lights, I asked her why she'd married Franz to begin with, was she in love with him, and she looked at me sadly and said she didn't remember now if she ever was, wasn't that the bee's knees?

I went into my own room after that and took out this picture I have of my father, my real and un-German one, who died when I was six in a car accident. I sat down at my desk and took it out of the CD case I keep it in and held it at the corners so I wouldn't vandalize it with fingerprints. In the picture, my dad and I are in a boat together, one of those ferries you can take to Alcatraz to avoid the sharks. He looks young and very smart in his glasses, and you can see this funny detail above the enormousness of his nose, how his eyebrows kind of join forces in a unibrow. I sat there at my desk and stared at the picture for a long time. Our hair is levitating from the wind, which seems very fierce and bone-chilling, and by the way I'm tucked into my father's lap it looks like he's protecting me from the cold.

The next evening, Colin and I went to Mr. Pizza Man so he could play pinball on his favorite machine, which had a scoreboard featuring women in costumes from the future and very true-to-breast cleavages. I sat in one of the booths, watching him dominate the machine with his perfect skills. Then we drove to the Church like always and parked in front of the big transformer with the sulfur lights brightening the sky and putting the stars out of business. He tried to pet me for a while, but I guess I wasn't in the mood because I didn't return his advances in a right-away fashion. He stopped advancing and frowned for a second and then looked at me seriously, his eyes shining in that weird way they had. That was when he told me about his secret powers. He made me promise not to tell anyone and then explained that he could see into the future before it happened, which was why he could play pinball forever without losing a coin. He knew the itinerary of the pinball before it occurred. I was very startled and didn't speak for a long time. I asked him if he could see into my future like the pinball's. He said, yes, he could see my whole life and even beyond that, but that the knowledge was in his body and the only way to share it was to pass it directly. The Gift, he called it. I didn't really believe him, but probably I was so in love with his Colinness that it didn't matter what was true or not. I thought for a long time, about how he used to be a sick boy with no power even to give his heart enough kilowatts to beat, and about how I thought of him twenty-four hours a day until I couldn't sleep, and how if I knew my future for real, I might stop being so scared about everything in this great and mysterious world founded by God—about my own helpless feeling and my mom being an unrecovering alcoholic and Jeanie being mentally ill when she used to be my friend—and then I told him that next Saturday, not the coming one but a week from then, December 18, 2004, I'd be ready in my room at 9:00 p.m. sharp.

That week, I was totally aside myself. I must have been wearing Colin Goggles that I couldn't remove because everywhere I looked he seemed to be coming toward me, kind of scary and beautiful-looking at the same time. I couldn't get him out of my thoughts. On Wednesday I went to Open School night with

Mom and Jeanie, which was very challenging because Jeanie and I weren't on one of our speaking terms and we had to meet all the teachers while pretending to be a happy family unpopulated by sluts and alcoholics. Perhaps, Mr. Patterson, you remember talking to us?[8] I kept looking around at the other families on the basketball court and seeing Colin's face attached to some distant boy's neck, even though I knew he wasn't coming on account of his own parents being in Hawaii. When the boy turned out to be a stranger, I'd Colinize someone else's face instead. There were about a million families all squeezed into the arena, and I watched all the married couples following behind their offspring or step-offspring and it suddenly seemed like Jeanie was right, like it was just some meaningless random thing who intercoursed who, like the moms and dads had just picked whoever was around because they were too lonely or desperate or sex-crazed to wait. It's really weird, but I had this Jeanie-ish idea like maybe we were in a giant barnyard.

When Saturday finally arrived, I couldn't wait all day in my room without becoming mentally ill myself, so I drove to the construction site in El Cerrito where Colin was working. It was a very warm day for December, and I parked behind a trailer where no one could see me. Colin was up there on top of the house he was building, kneeling like a Japanese person and hammering nails into a two-by-four made of wood. A radio on

---

[8]YOU: Hi, Maria. This must be your mother.
MOM (*drunk since dinner*): He doesn't look like your dad one bit. Where do you see it? He looks like a teacher!
YOU: Ha ha ha. Maybe I should get a tattoo or something to disguise myself better.
JEANIE (*smirking*): **Natalie**'s got a tattoo. My sister, **Natalie**. Go ahead and show it, **Natalie**.
YOU: Wow. Look at that. (*lifting your glasses*) A microwave?
ME: It's a cobra.
YOU: Gosh.

the ground was blasting hard rock from the eighties, all metal all the time, so I don't think anyone heard me pull up. It was kind of weird that Colin was working, because I saw the other guys on the crew taking their lunch break on the gates of their pickups in a very chummy manner. Colin had his shirt off, and when I first saw him from the back, the way his muscles kind of remained invisible until he bent down to hammer a nail and they came up like a secret promise to Natalie Mudbrook, a volt of longing went through me and all my doubts about intercourse were exploded. It didn't matter to me that I was only 99 percent sure of his devotion. I fantasized that Colin and I were already married and that he was building us a house, a big beautiful mansion where we could live out our days in endless eternity.

And then something very strange occurred. This woman walked by in one of those running tops that show your belly button, walking a big dog in front of her, and the crew started yelling at her in this very discriminating manner. They were wiggling their tongues and making their hammers into phallic symbols and even performing air intercourse. I glanced up at Colin and wondered if he'd come to her rescue, because I knew he was very respecting of women. Instead, he put his hand on his sewn-up heart and called her a *mamacita* in Spanish and asked for her phone number in this loud voice that everyone could hear. Of course, I knew that he was just trying to impress his co-workers, that he didn't really want the little mama's number at all, but it gave me this weird feeling like my own heart was struggling to beat.

I left the construction site and drove around for a long time, sort of without knowing where I was going, like a ghost or something, until finally I stopped at a random Burger King for a Pepsi. I sat in one of the booths by myself and stared through the open window at the neon sign, which said HOME OF THE

WHOPPER in big buzzing letters. I remember thinking how everything was supposed to have a home, even the Whopper, but what if you weren't the Whopper but just a girl whose mom and stepfather couldn't get along and everyone you saw or loved—even a beautiful boy you were about to intercourse in a couple hours—seemed to belong to a secret home somewhere you couldn't find? I mean it was out there, but no one had bothered to tell you where it was? So you had to go and sit in the Whopper's home instead, like a burglar.

When it was dark, I drove around some more to unwind my head and then went up the back way of the house like always, passing by Jeanie's room on the way to my own. I was feeling a desperate need to talk to her and started to knock on her door, but then I heard her plowing her slutdom and froze in midknock. I pressed my ear against the door. Jeanie was talking to someone in a strange voice, kind of loud and whispery at the same time, like she was trying to melt an ice cube in her teeth. Now and then a deep voice would interrupt her in a very personal fashion. It wasn't a slut-a-thon, I realized, but just a conversation. Then the deep voice said something and she laughed. It was a woman's laugh, ungirl-like and beautiful. The weird thing is, I felt kind of jealous. Not because I wanted to be a full-time premier slut, or because a boy had never made me laugh like that—but because I wanted to be the one making her laugh. Then whoever it was she was talking to got up and walked around and I lost my breath for a minute, because his shuffles were united with a faint sort of jingling, like coins.

I went to my room and lay in bed, trying not to think about nine o'clock almost arriving. It was storming pretty hard outside, and for some reason I thought about all those turkeys stuck out in the rain, all soaked and miserable, drowning maybe because they didn't know enough to get out of it. It made me very sad. There was this little worm of rain moving on the window, kind of wriggling for no reason, and I watched it for a long time.

Then I heard a knock and the room's energy changed completely. The energy collected around my body and seeped into my own skin too, like I was a giant battery getting charged. Everything seemed connected: the rain squirming, my heart pounding, the earth turning on its axle. Colin opened the door. He looked more beautiful than I'd ever seen him, face glowing with confidence and his hair kind of floating around him like a commercial. His clothes were only a little damp, despite the undry weather. I was very scared. He walked over to the bed and knelt beside my face. He didn't say a word, just reached down and touched my lips, which made my eyelids sparkle at a very high frequency. I knew I wouldn't stop him from transmitting me the Gift. He stood up all of a sudden and walked over to the window—I guess to close the curtains so no one would witness my conduction. His jeans were kind of slipping down like usual, and I could see this strip of skin below his tan line that was all bumpy and wrinkled from the elastic force of his boxers. I imagined it was one of those Braille messages for blind people to touch that said BELOW THIS LINE IS THE REST OF YOUR LIFE.

But just as Colin was turning around to come back to bed, we heard a sound on the stairs that sounded like my mother's coughing lungs. This was very unusual, because she almost never came to visit me, and when she did it was generally during the daytime when I wasn't being deflowered. But sure enough, her steps began coming up the stairs. For a second, I just lay there like an embalmed person. Then I grabbed Colin's arm and put him in the closet, telling him to wait there until the coast was cleared.

I was glad to see my mom wasn't completely drunk yet, because she didn't have the sniffling nose and bare feet she got when she was inebriated. There was just a frizz of gray hair like a piece of tinsel hanging into her eyes for Christmas. She walked over to the bed and looked at me with a sad expression. She said she was sorry, and I said what for? and she didn't say anything but just kind of looked around the room, like she sensed Colin's energy. Then she bent down and hugged me. I held her back and didn't let go right away. Her hair was soft, and I could smell the maximum dandruff control of the Head & Shoulders she uses. She said, My god, sweetie, you're trembling like a leaf. I wanted to ask her some questions about what it was like to be a full-grown woman with gray hairs in your face. Like, had a man ever solved her problems even for a week? Was being a woman, at least, something to look forward to? But I didn't. I just hugged her until I could feel her heart beating through my sweater. I was squeezing pretty hard because she eventually had to peel my arms from her neck on account of her historic back trouble.

And then she left, except I didn't tell Colin that she was gone right away. Instead I just lay there by myself and thought about this song Jeanie and I used to sing, the one with the double intenders in it. "Miss Lucy," it was called. I lip-synched it in my head, picturing us under our favorite tree and clapping each other's hands in a fast-motion rhythm like we used to:

> Ask me no more questions, I'll tell you no more lies,
> The boys are in the bedroom, pulling down their . . .
> Flies are in the meadow, bees are in the park,
> The boys and girls are kissing in the . . .
> D-A-R-K
> D-A-R-K
> D-A-R-K
> Dark
> Dark
> Dark

When I was a kid, I always loved the ending, how you spelled out "dark" with all its letters, like you didn't want the song to end and spelling the last word was a way of putting it off for as long as you could. Sometimes, when my mom used to tuck me into bed, I tried to do the same thing in actual life and spell out the words of whatever I saw in my room, saying the letters in my brain, like it could maybe stop her from leaving and turning off the lights. C-L-O-S-E-T. There was a noise against the door, like the rustle-around of an animal. C-L-O-S-E-T. Soon I would know everything. C-L-O-S-E-T. I stared at the thing I didn't want to say, listening for Colin's breath behind the door, trying in my wildest brain to imagine what he'd look like when it opened.

Love exists. It has to.

I'm sorry, Mr. Patterson. I know I'm going to fail this essay, and probably the whole course, but it seems like William Butler Yeats has a lot of very talented groupies to explain his poem—but who's ever going to explain my story except me? Who'd ever waste their precious time to sign up for Natalie Mudbrook 101?

It's been two months now since Jeanie and Colin disappeared. Franz thinks they were in a conspiracy and ran off together, but perhaps it's just an accident that they vanished at the same time. My mom and Franz filed a Missing Jeanie report with the police, even though her duffel bag is gone and she clearly packed up her own things because she remembered to take Hippo with her. Some guys at school say that Colin kidnapped her and took advantage of her mental unfitness, or else that they're both crazy and made a suicide pact like those Davidist people in Texas. But I try not to listen to anyone else. Sometimes I think about Colin's face that night after we'd become single backs again, when it wasn't so wild and unhuman but more like a little boy's in the hospital, looking sad and far off and not known by anyone—which was the way I was feeling too. On the weekends, I drive out to the construction site where he used to work and watch the crew nailing our house together. I just sit there in the car, watching it get taller every week. Sometimes I close my eyes for sixty seconds like a game, imagining that when I open them again I'll see Colin walking toward me with his long hair and tool belt and glowing tan arms, the house finished and waiting to be peopled with newlyweds, like a movie version of my destiny.

But the weird thing is, with my eyes closed, I don't see Colin at all. I see Jeanie's brown eyes and size-challenged nose, which aren't the movie features I was thinking about. We're sitting in the half-built house, all hunched together because of the wind, pulling candlesticks and egg slicers and curtain-tier-uppers out of a pillowcase. Our eyes are crying at the beautiful objects. That's how I know Jeanie's really just run off like an orphan, except this time for real—that she's waiting under a tree somewhere, living out of her duffel like a duffel bag-lady, except I don't know where.

Other times, I drive up to the city and hang out in the park, watching the ducks and swans swim around in the little lake next to the paddleboat dock. The swans are very peaceful and not at all like William Butler Yeats describes in his poetry. Perhaps they have "strange hearts," but how would you know without performing surgery?[9] I've never actually seen the swans intercourse, but I can tell that their mating habits are not perverted or interracial when it comes to humans. I look at how beautiful they are with their swan-shaped bodies and necks like question marks and imagine that there's a daughter growing inside of me already. I know I'll have a girl because of the Gift,

---

[9] Unless by "strange" he means like everyone else's and therefore alone under their swanny feathers, in which case I'm not going to argue with that.

which gets stronger and more giftlike every day. For example, I know she's going to be very beautiful, like Helen Troy, who launched a thousand ships with her face. I know for certain that no one will ever want to disappear without telling her. And I know just as certainly that she'll be famous and worshipped in the chests of strangers, that men will fight over her and even meet tragic endings.

Meanwhile, Franz hides in the TV room after dinner, and my mom complains to me every night while I tuck her in, and the elm in the backyard where Jeanie and I used to play is invested with bugs.

I wonder, Mr. Patterson, if you can change something that's not assembled yet. If you know the future, can you keep it from happening? The Gift is very strong, but actually it hasn't come all at once like you'd think. Instead, I'll be sitting in European history class with my eyes half-closed from boredom, or just staring out the window of my room while Tamara bitches about Tamara on the phone, and suddenly I'll see a whole scene flash through my head, a perfect smellable dream-picture except I'm awake, like I could walk into my own brain and take a photograph. Sometimes they're people I don't recognize, but usually it's someone I know pretty well or at least have seen before in my regular life. I'm trying to make sense of the dream-pictures as they come. Like my mom with a black eye and slippers on her feet, hiding on the roof of our house while it's raining out. Or Rogelio, the school janitor, staring out the window of an airplane with his hands trembling a little bit under the tray table in its unlocked and downright position. Or one that I've seen more than once, which is Jeanie lying totally alone in an apartment somewhere without furniture, her ear pressed to the rug and listening to music through the floor. She's wearing one of her extra-small T-shirts with stains under the arms, like maybe she hasn't changed it for a while, but she's smiling with this little-girl look like the music is the Secret of Everything and making her extremely happy, reminding her of something else, like maybe the secret really has to do with the *past* and not the future, but I can't get close enough in my head to hear it.

Or sometimes even you, Mr. Patterson. Take right now, for example. I can see you sitting in your office at school, reading this essay before I'm even finished with it. You're holding a coffee mug that says: READ BANNED BOOKS. Your office is very cold and sweet-smelling, because you just finished smoking a pipe filled with illicit marijuana buds that you hide in your glasses case (you blew the smoke out the window to prevent your being narced on by another teacher's nose). I've never noticed from the back row of class, but your eyebrows kind of connect into one. I see that you're wondering, as you read, how much you smoked. That the hair on the back of your neck is tingling. That you're finishing my essay. Right this second. And that you might even know now who I am.

Child's Play

C. P. PITTS SLID DOWN THE BAN-
ister in a way that was strictly forbidden,
starting near the top of the stairs where the landing was, where
the railing sloped gently and deceptively before tilting down the
steps like the dip of a roller coaster, his bangs lifting from his eyes
as he picked up speed and began a hurtling course downward,
growing more and more alarmed at the slideability of his new
Levi's, leaping off before the banister curled into a snake coil,
and avoiding—in his five-second descent—a 35 percent chance
of falling over backward and breaking his neck. He whooped.
He yelled his name. He pumped his fist in victory and danced to
the amplified riffs of Deep Purple throbbing from his stepbrother's room upstairs. Smoke on the water! Fire in the sky!
He played air guitar without knowing a single chord, wiggling
the fingers of his left hand as if he had an insatiable itch on his
stomach. So what if his penis was deformed? So what if he had

only one friend, Everett Hazelrigg, whom everyone called "The Alien" because he'd laughed so hard while drinking Mountain Dew that it shot out of one eye? So what if he'd been playing in the backyard with Everett a month ago and his stepbrother had found them stripped mysteriously to their B.V.D.s, fencing with plastic swords, and his stepbrother had bowed at the waist and said in a British accent: *I hereby dub thee the Fagaholic Knights*?

C.P. banged into the kitchen, startling his mother as she breast-fed the Angry Demon Who Screamed at His Face. The baby's head was pink and glowing, poking from a yellow blanket wrapped fiercely around its body. It looked like a giant peanut. C.P.'s mother flashed him a look over the baby's head, a tight slimming of the lips that he'd come to identify in the past two months as the what's-wrong-with-you-you-might-disturb-the-baby look.

"Hey, Mom," he said quietly, in his new baby-proof voice, "is my Halloween costume ready?"

"God, that's right," she said, studying the peanut in her lap. She was always staring at the baby's head. "What is it again? A homicidal mute person?"

"Mutant! With radioactive flesh."

"I don't know, dear. It's been a crazy day already. Can you get your brother to help you?"

C.P. looked at her in distress. His stepbrother was still finishing his own costume, supposedly—something called a "69 Position," which involved an upside-down mannequin in high heels belted to his waist. He'd shown it to C.P. under a death threat of secrecy. "Halloween's in *six hours*."

"I'll have to go through the basement. As soon as I have a minute."

C.P. frowned, kicking his sneaker against the floor so it chirped. "So, like, are you going to be using the kitchen for a long time?"

"I don't know, honey," she said, looking at him. "I hadn't thought about it. Why do you ask?"

"There are some guys coming over. From the neighborhood. I thought you might want to be by yourself or something."

"Don't be silly. I don't mind. As long as they don't cause an earthquake." His mother's face turned serious, as if she were tweezing a splinter. "Is Everett Hazelrigg coming?"

He shrugged. Everett had been his best friend since second grade, but they hadn't been seeing each other as much as they used to. To be honest, C.P. was starting to become a little embarrassed by their friendship. For example, why couldn't Everett just laugh normally, rather than exploding in a giant snorting fit when he was supposed to be swallowing his lunch? "He's busy, I think."

"You should be nice to him, Clinton Parker," his mother said sternly, wiping a disgusting vein of milk from the baby's chin. "Everett needs you right now—more than your new buddies, no matter how much they like you."

C.P. ambled over to the fridge, opening it for no particular reason other than to take a look at its contents, which he inventoried about every fifteen minutes or so in case a spectacular event had vaporized the shelves' offerings and replaced them with something edible. He loved his mother, but she had begun to humiliate him terribly. It was bad enough that she insisted on asking about Everett during car pool whenever he missed a day of school, getting that same serious look and referring to him as C.P.'s "bosom buddy," so that the boys in the backseat plucked their shirts out in the Universal Boob Language and pretended to suckle themselves. Far worse was the actual suckling, the baby feeding that meant she was always showing her big boob in public, exposing the oozy thing in the kitchen or outside on the porch with it sticking out of her blouse for everyone to see. And in fact everyone did see it—all the kids in the neighborhood, at least—because they'd suddenly started visiting C.P. out of the blue, coming by on the weekends in a pack of three or four or five, telling his mom politely that they'd come to play Stratego or jump on the trampoline or help him move bricks into the backyard. Of course, his mom thought it was great that he was making friends in the neighborhood. Could he say: *Actually, Mom, they're here to see your boob?* That they—these *nice and pleasant friends*—called her Mrs. Tits and Leaky Boobs and Her Royal Udder, mooing like a cow every time he had to run home for dinner? That his own name had been transformed, permanently perhaps, to Seepy Tits—as in, *Hey, Seepy Tits, could you spare some milk?*

He shut the door to the fridge, disgusted by the lack of soda products. The lack was only an example of a larger unfairness, a link in an Earth-spannable chain of unfairnesses, just like he wasn't allowed to eat Ding Dongs or play Butt's Up in the driveway or watch *CHiPs* before bed like the rest of his neighbors, because his parents were liberals who didn't believe in junk food or violence but liked to show everyone their boob. C.P. turned and caught the baby's attention, surprising it by accident. He tried his best to smile. The baby immediately burst into a scream, its tiny face squirming into a mask of fury.

"C.P., don't scare her! Now look what you've done."

The boys marched down Wendover Road, armed with a variety of weapons: Freddy Neubaumer, alias Stink Baum, wielding an authentic, frontier-era rifle with real cocking trigger-guard action and smoke curls decorating the stock, bought by his father at the Frontierland shop in Disneyland during spring vacation, a trip distinguished by his grandpa's insistence on calling him Dudley, the numinous, half-second glimpse of a blow job in his hotel room whenever he switched to Channel 28, and the tremendous stink of his feet after walking around the Magic Kingdom in ninety-three-degree sun and no socks; Moby Florence, alias Flo or occasionally Flo Man, wielding a machine gun with a detachable bipod and real, battery-powered sound effects—a *huhuhuhuhuhuhuh* when you pressed the trigger— one of many gifts he'd opened a week before last Christmas while his parents were gone and then rewrapped as best he could with foot-long strips of Scotch tape, so that his presents on Christmas morning resembled the work of deranged elves; Kevin Webster, alias Webbie, wielding a German Luger with a broken trigger and removable plastic magazine, long since lost, all sound effects created by Kevin himself, be it blasting some- one's face into a tree *(pakow)*, braining him from behind with a silencer *(pyeeew)*, or sending his knees across the street like hockey pucks *(pa-ching, pa-chang)*; and Barker Beemis, no alias required, wielding a Colt .45 revolver that you could load with rings of caps, one of which he'd started wearing on his pinkie as a secret pact with God, concerned about the eternal conse- quences of jerking off, which he kept vowing he'd never in a trillion years try again while picturing Mrs. Pitts's breast—or something terrible would happen to them both.

They moved slowly, squeezing the guns at their sides. The neighborhood itself showed evidence of marauders, though what kind it was hard to say. Pumpkins lay smashed on the doorstep of the Websters' house, swarming with flies. At the Ballieres', egg trails slimed down the windows and glistened in the sun. The Linaweavers' had been TPed everywhere with red crepe paper, so that the big ginkgo tree in the front yard seemed to wiggle with flames whenever a breeze swept through it. The boys took in the damage without commenting, mostly because they'd discussed it already and their minds had drifted else- where, stuck on their new and favorite hobby, which was interpreting the names of sports teams literally and then pitting them against each other in endless permutations.

"What about the Dolphins versus the Lions?"

"Lion meat. A massacre."

"Dolphins are smart, though. They talk to each other."

"So what?"

"They could organize an ambush."

"It's Astroturf, dumbshit. They can't move."

"Okay, here's one. Here's one. Giants versus the Jets."

"Are you talking Godzilla size or Jolly Green?"

"Who cares? The jets would fly into their eyes and blind them. A blind giant is worse than a dolphin."

"Giants don't need eyes. They can smell your blood. *I smell the blood of an Englishman.*"

"Okay. Wait a second. Padres versus the Vikings."

"What's a padre?"

"Like a Mexican priest."

"Do they have guns?"

"Sure. All Mexicans have guns."

"Doesn't matter. Any Viking on Earth could kick a priest's ass."

"Aren't Vikings, like, pagans? Priests could pray for their deaths? Like a plague or something?"

They stopped at the end of the block and fell quiet, reconnoitering the Pittses' house. The street was eerily deserted, and the way the trees swayed in the wind made them clutch their guns to keep warm. How to proceed? Maple samaras coptered from the sky. Freddy began to make a sound, a low moan, as if he were in pain or misery or worse—dying, perhaps—and then Barker and Kevin and Moby joined in, four boys mooing on the street.

• • •

C.P. heard something outside, like zombies moaning because they hadn't eaten enough brains, but then laughed it off because zombies didn't exist—ha ha ha!—though if you *were* a zombie, wouldn't Halloween be the optimum time to come out since no one would recognize you and everyone would open their doors to your brain-eating delight? He looked at the grandfather clock in the living room. It dawned on him that he'd never get to be a Homicidal Mutant, that—just like all the years before—his mom would wait until five o'clock before realizing she had no materials for a costume and start cursing under her breath and end up painting his entire body with a mixture of Crisco and food coloring, passing him off as a giant fruit. Last year, she'd painted C.P. yellow and stuffed him with pillows to look like a lemon, but several people had thought he was a speed bump.

The doorbell rang. He ran out of the living room and surfed partway on the Oriental rug lining the foyer before ditching it, expertly, at the door. To avoid the infamy of any new nicknames, he placed himself in front of the bowl of toothbrushes his mom planned to hand out for Halloween. Enter C.P.'s neighbors, greeting him with guns. They moved toward the pantry. C.P. zipped in front of the door and stood there with his back to it.

"Where's your mom?" Freddy asked.

"She went out," C.P. said.

"But your car's here. I saw it in the driveway."

C.P. felt himself blush. "Actually, she's upstairs. But she can't see anyone. She's sick."

"Sick?"

"She's got polio."

Kevin narrowed his eyes. "I thought only kids got that."

"Isn't that the baby?" Moby asked, poking his machine gun at the pantry door. "I can hear it screaming."

"Sure. It misses my mom. Her milk's all contaminated and she can't take care of it."

"So who's feeding it?"

"My grandma," said C.P.—forced, for the first time, to imagine his grandmother's breast. The image stuck in his brain like a piece of gum, waiting to be rediscovered. "She's visiting from Wisconsin."

His neighbors looked at him while the Angry Demon screamed from the kitchen. Why *polio,* for Christ sake? Why couldn't he have said the flu? A cold? A bad case of poison oak? They glanced at each other, trading smirks—everyone, that is, except for Barker, who'd met his mom only twice but looked extremely upset, as if someone had kneed him in the stomach. He stared at the cap ring on his pinkie. "Did your mom get sick, like, recently?"

"All right," Kevin said, still smirking. "You've probably got a lot to do then. Polio stuff, right? We don't want to intrude."

They turned, heading for the door.

"Where are you going?" C.P. asked.

"The Battle of Hallows' Eve," Freddy said. "Last man standing."

"Can I play?"

The four boys glanced at each other again. "You don't have a gun," Kevin said scornfully.

It was true. His parents refused to buy him anything remotely gunlike, which was why he still pranced around with plastic swords. "I know where a real gun is," C.P. said.

"Bullshit," Freddy said.

"I'm serious. Everett Hazelrigg's dad. The Alien." He shrugged, trying to downplay it. "He used to be a Green Beret."

"You're full of it."

"It's in the attic. He stole it from a dead person—an actual real pistol, that shoots."

He let the words hang there, savoring the looks on his neighbors' faces. He'd promised not to tell anyone about the gun, promised Everett through a long and complicated series of heart-swears and Sacred Pee-Stream Crossings, but he was too excited to feel any guilt about it. It wasn't like Everett had been the all-time greatest friend lately himself. He'd begun staying inside on weekends for no good reason, saying that his mom required his services around the house—that was what he said, "required his services"—or leaving school after lunch with a signed excuse from P.E., so that now C.P. was actually the *last* one picked for soccer or beam ball or floor hockey amid a frog chorus of groans. And then there was the new problem with Everett's head, namely that it was balding in one place like Friar Tuck's because he couldn't help pulling out his own hair in class, harvesting a pink coin of scalp that shrank or widened mysteriously from week to week. "Trichotillomania," Everett called it. It was stuff like this that made C.P. so embarrassed at school.

But when it was just the two of them, C.P. really liked hanging out with Everett. They were always doing fun things that made them laugh, like fencing in their underwear, which C.P. had thought was pretty damn hilarious himself, until his stepbrother had found them and he felt ashamed and faggoty and furious at Everett, though (truth be told) it was C.P.'s idea to begin with. Or else, before Everett's mom began napping all the time, they'd kick back in his room doing nothing in particular, staring at all the cool tropical fish his dad had bought him, the guppies and black mollies and silver hatchets. There were so many fish he needed two tanks to hold them all. When they were younger, they used to go there after Sunday School and play Nazareth, a game they'd invented after reading a comic book about Jesus. C.P. and Everett would take turns closing their eyes and trying to perform their own miracles, such as squeezing blood from a rock or turning a glass of tap water into wine. Once, inspired by Jesus' resurrection of Lazarus, they captured a lizard in Everett's backyard and then stuck it in the freezer in a piece of Tupperware, waiting an hour or so until the thing was frozen into a corpse. But when they tried to resurrect it—Everett holding the lizard in his fist, muttering a prayer, and commanding *Lizardus, come forth!* before opening his hand—it just lay there dead as a stick, its little tail shattered into bits.

But now here C.P. was, First Lieutenant Pitts, leading the coolest guys on the block down to Everett's place so he could show them a real and actual pistol. They turned down Adelaide Street and walked until they reached the Hazelriggs', the only house on the block not decked out with Halloween decorations. There were leaves covering the front lawn, millions of them, as if Mr. Hazelrigg was on a dad strike against fall. C.P. knocked on the door while his neighbors waited behind him. He tried to imagine what he'd say to Everett's mom, a plump woman with freakish red hair down to her waist. C.P. hadn't seen her—not once—since summer.

Luckily it was Everett who opened the door, his own red hair flattened to his scalp as if he hadn't showered in a while. Even though it was the weekend, he was wearing the same thing as always: a pair of ironed khakis and a purple corduroy shirt that their teacher, Mrs. Sissel, had once called "dashing."

"I brought some friends over," C.P. said. "They want to see your room."

"My room?"

"They've never seen it."

Everett stared at them. He seemed amazed that C.P. was no longer a Fagaholic Knight and hung out with normal people who didn't jump around in their underwear. "It's Saturday. I'm pretty busy."

"Is your dad around?" Kevin said, bumping his way into the house.

"He's at the store. Buying groceries." Everett glanced behind him. "My mom's asleep—I'm not allowed to have people over."

C.P.'s neighbors ignored him, filing into the house after Kevin and squinting around the front hall with skeptical looks. Who'd ever heard of a Green Beret buying groceries? Everett turned to follow and C.P. stared at the back of his head, which was balder than he'd ever seen it. He wondered if Everett was actually going bald for real, like those kids who look like they're sixty and get sent to Disneyland all expenses paid for their dying wish.

"What's the deal?" Freddy said, still examining the front hall. "How come you don't have any Halloween decorations?"

"We're not celebrating." Everett turned to C.P., speaking in a different voice. "Look, you're really not supposed to be over."

"Why aren't you giving out candy?" Barker asked.

He blushed. "My dad doesn't want to."

"Man, Naziville. Iron hand. So what are you going to be for Halloween?"

"A human," Moby said under his breath, which caused Freddy to snicker.

Everett didn't seem to hear. "I'm not dressing up."

"What do you mean?"

"It's dumb. The whole thing. I'm not going trick-or-treating."

The group was silent. "Alien," mouthed Freddy, lifting his eyes toward the ceiling. Moby, Barker, and Kevin stood in the front hall, inspecting a painting of Everett's mother sitting on a horse. She looked much younger in the painting, her red hair tied up in a fancy knot on top of her head. Everett waited by the plastic-covered sofa, glancing up the stairs every few seconds and plucking at his bald spot. Now that he was inside the house, C.P. thought about his own mother's serious-looking face whenever she mentioned Everett, the way her eyes crinkled into older ones. It gave him a weird feeling, as if a bowl of his mom's oatmeal (Lumpis Cementum, his stepbrother called it) had glued itself to his stomach. He was about to suggest they forget about the gun and go back outside when Kevin started to clomp upstairs with Barker and Moby and Freddy following at his heels.

"C.P., tell them," Everett said desperately, standing by the couch. "They can't go upstairs."

The four of them stopped and looked at C.P., waiting for an answer. The oatmeal in his stomach had hardened into something heavier. He thought about what would happen if he told everyone to leave, the herd-sound of moos that would follow him home.

"We'll take our shoes off," C.P. said, refusing to look at Everett.

Reluctantly, the four boys sat down on the steps, following C.P.'s command and grumbling about the stench of Freddy's feet. Everett stood there without moving. Then he snapped out of his trance and squeezed ahead of the boys on the stairs, crouching by as if they weren't even there. By the time they got to his room, edging past the sign on the door—EVERETT'S LAIR, which caused Freddy to snicker again—C.P. wished they'd never come over. The room looked different than he remembered it. The walls, which two months ago had been plastered with Beatles posters, were completely bare except for the black velvet painting of a unicorn hanging above Everett's bed. The unicorn was standing atop a snow-covered mountain, rearing its legs in the moonlight. In the back of the room, near the record player, was a single fish tank containing only a few measly pencil fish and a black molly hidden between the legs of a little burping skeleton in the corner. A dead guppy lay at the top of the tank, floating like a twig.

"Boy," Barker said. "What a faggy poster." He looked at

Everett, squishing his words into baby talk. "Is that your special unicorn?"

Kevin flashed him a look. "Unicorns are cool. They screw virgins with their horns."

"What?"

"That's what my brother told me. Virgin screwers." He winked at Barker. "If she's not a virgin, they'll impale her to death instead."

"There used to be Beatles posters," C.P. said, feeling the need to defend Everett. "A KISS one too. Gene Simmons, with his tongue on fire." He wasn't sure about this last image, but it sounded pretty cool.

"What happened to them?"

Everett looked down at his lap. "My mom made me take them down. After John Lennon got shot."

C.P. could tell he was making this up, because Everett's face always turned red whenever he was lying. For whatever reason, he'd taken the posters down himself.

"So what about the gun?" Freddy asked.

Everett stared at C.P., the redness evaporating from his face.

"I told them about your dad," C.P. said quietly. "How he was a Green Beret and everything."

Everett looked away, wincing as if he was caught in a flashlight. For a second, C.P. worried that he might retaliate with a best-friend secret of his own, some sworn confession that C.P. had made, like how his penis hooked leftward in an erect state and would probably require a corrective penis cast if he ever wanted to have sex. "He wasn't a Green Beret," Everett whispered. "I just said that. He was a correspondent for the newspaper."

"But there's a gun, right?" Moby said.

"No. I mean, it's in the attic. We can't go up there or we'll wake my mom."

"You go up," Kevin said sweetly. "Go up quietly and then bring it down and show us."

Everett shook his head. The boys looked at C.P. again, which made him feel cool and lieutenanty but also like he wanted to sneak out the window and shinny down the oak in Everett's backyard. Instead, he coaxed Everett from the room and they stood there in the hall, right outside the door. C.P. looked off again to avoid Everett's eyes. He felt angry but couldn't defend it or even say why—which made him angrier still.

"They were making fun of you," C.P. said confidentially, "calling you 'Alien.' That's why I told them."

"You shouldn't have," Everett said. His voice sounded thin and eggshelly.

"We don't care about sports or shooting people, right? This way you can show them. How stupid their guns are."

Everett chewed his lip, as if he wanted to believe C.P. but wasn't a hundred percent sure. He glanced behind him and then made C.P. latch fingers with their thumbs pressed together in a mutual Fonzie before heading up to the attic. It was the secret handshake they'd used when they were seven, to prove their allegiance to the Nazareth Redeemers. C.P. walked back into the room, glad no one had seen it. The boys eyed him suspiciously over their plastic weapons, and he suddenly felt alone and alien-like, his anger at Everett leaking away. Maybe C.P. hadn't been lying to him after all.

When Everett came back, he was carrying a metal box that looked like one of those things you keep fishing lures in. He unlatched the buckles on the box and opened it and pulled out the gun, which was wrapped carefully in a white cloth. A hush came over the room. Everett removed the cloth like a bandage, unwrapping it until the gun was shining in his hand, a beautiful pistol with a scratched-up barrel and a hammer too large to cock with your thumb. There was a red star embossed in the middle of the grip. C.P. could tell, by the looks on everyone's faces, that the sight of it made their own guns pointless.

They sat on the bed and took turns holding it, passing it to one another as if it might escape from their fingers. It was so heavy that C.P. held it with two hands. The gun smelled sweet and musty at the same time, like the boxes of raisins C.P.'s mother stuck in his lunch.

"Who would you kill?" Kevin asked finally—a whisper.

"What do you mean?"

"I mean, if you could kill anyone. To be famous like Mark David Chapman. Who would it be?"

There was a long silence. Moby, who'd finished looking at the gun, laid it tenderly on the pillow. "My little brother. No contest."

"Mrs. Sissel."

"My stepmom? Maybe, like, John Denver?"

"What about you, Everett?" Kevin asked. "Who would you kill to be famous?"

Everett stood up. C.P. thought he'd be proud of the gun's effect, but something about the conversation seemed to bother him. His face was weird and damp-looking, and his hand was twisting the leg of his khakis, probably to keep it from getting at his head.

"No one," he said.

Freddy snorted. "So how are you going to be famous?"

"I can do miracles."

C.P.'s heart plunged into his stomach. Everyone stared at Everett. Barker made a Twilight Zone noise while wiggling his fingers.

"What kind of miracles?" Kevin said, straight-faced.

Everett looked around the room, as if he were trying to remember himself. "I can rescue things from the dead."

"Hoo man," Freddy said. "That's it. He's gone bugfuck."

"That guppy. The dead one, see it?" He pointed to the fish tank by the record player. "I can bring it back to life."

"Bullshit."

"Freakland. You're a freak of all freaks."

"Let's see it," Kevin said.

Everett closed his eyes for a second and took a deep breath. He looked at C.P. "It's a bet. If I do it, you guys have to leave me and C.P. alone. No more making fun of us." He narrowed his eyes. "You have to treat us with respect. And pick us first for whatever game you're playing. And serve us lunch, like waiters, all next week at school."

"And what if you *don't*?"

He shrugged. "Your decision. Whatever you want."

"If not," Kevin said, speaking for everyone to hear, "we get to give you the Alien Treatment."

C.P. stared at Everett, whose face was very serious and churchlike, as though maybe it had caught on a single expression and couldn't uncatch. Everett went to the bathroom for a minute to wash his hands—important for miracle-making—then came out again and walked over to the fish tank. He opened the lid and reached into the tank and trapped the dead guppy in his fist. He bowed his head, as if he were praying, then turned around after a minute so that everyone could see him. He closed his eyes and held his fist in front of him and began to whisper in a made-up language, his face lifted toward the ceiling. It was the way he and C.P. used to talk when they were alone, except stranger even and more fagaholic-sounding. This time, though, when Everett opened his hand and nothing had happened, there'd be four other people in the room waiting to make fun of them.

Everett finished his whispering and kissed his fist once and then opened his fingers one at a time. The guppy lay there in his palm, deader than ever. Then it twitched its tail and started to flip around in Everett's hand as if it might jump out.

The room was silent. Everett walked back to the fish tank and stuck his fist in the water and the guppy swam from his hand, darting toward the side of the tank. Moby, who was standing next to C.P., began to sniff quietly, crying without making any noise from his throat.

"It's a miracle," Freddy said finally.

"Holy shit," Barker said. He glanced at Everett. "'Shoot,' I mean."

"That's impossible," Kevin said angrily. His face was red. He inspected the fish tank carefully, eyes peeled on the reborn guppy as if he were waiting for it to keel over again. Then he began to snoop around the room, peering behind things and lifting the scorpion domed in glass on the dresser and even hunting through Everett's drawers before ending up in the bathroom.

"Christ! Hey! There's another tank right here! With guppies." He stormed out, breathless. "There's a second tank in the bathroom. Hey, open his hand! The other one!"

Barker grabbed Everett and held him by the wrist of his left hand, which was squeezed into a fist. He tried to wriggle free, but Barker held him in a vise grip and then Kevin pried open his fingers, digging under them with his own. The dead guppy lay there in Everett's palm, squished into a greenish pulp.

"You switched them! Liar!"

"No, I didn't."

"Don't be stupid. You lost the bet."

"I didn't lose," Everett said.

"What do you mean, you little suck," Freddy said. "Deal's a deal. We get to give you the Alien Treatment."

"I didn't lose," he said, glaring. "You have to bring us lunch."

Moby, who'd stopped crying, picked up the gun from its

place on the pillow and pointed it at Everett's head. The pistol made Moby's hand look small and flimsy.

"Lie down on the bed. Fair's fair."

Everett looked at C.P., as if he were waiting for him to do something. Then he lay down on the bed without a fight, stretching onto his stomach. The bald spot on his head shone pink in the sunlight from the window.

"Aliens get the treatment," Moby said, trembling in a way you could hear in his breath. He was still pointing the gun at Everett's head. "Better known as the Prell Booster. Get the shampoo out of the bathroom, Kevin?"

Everyone was quiet. It was Kevin who usually gave the orders, but something had changed, a new hush in the room that made them all equal. Everett stared at C.P. from the bed, his face smooshed into the mattress. His eyes were open, but it was like they were stuck that way and he was looking at C.P. because he didn't have a choice. Why didn't he struggle? Help himself? Why was he such an all-time wuss that he couldn't defend himself and not stare at C.P. with those stuck-open eyes? Kevin laughed once—a weird laugh, as if he'd stubbed his toe— and then went into the bathroom and came out with a thing of shampoo, not Prell but some other kind, a bottle of fluorescent blue goop with the cap missing. Kevin's face was pale and strange, his lips tucked in so you couldn't see them. C.P. glanced at Barker and then Freddy: they both looked the same as Kevin did, scared and excited at the same time.

"Hold him down," Kevin said.

Freddy and Barker came over and pinned Everett's shoulders and legs, pressing him to the bed, though he wasn't moving at all and didn't seem to even care about escaping. He was still staring at C.P., his eyes refusing to look away or even blink.

"Your mom's an ugly cow," Everett said in a half whisper. "Cow tit. Her fat cow tit's going to fall off."

He started to make a sound, an ugly noise that began in his throat and came out his mouth without his lips moving at all. A mooing. C.P. went over to the bed and helped Kevin grab Everett's khakis and pull them down his legs, so that his ass was bare and everyone could see how white and scrawny and stupid-looking it was. There was a pimple on it, a single red bump sitting there large as a bumblebee. It seemed like the most private thing in the world. C.P. stared at it. Kevin took the shampoo bottle and stuck it inside of Everett and squeezed it until Everett stopped mooing. When he pulled it out, half the bottle was gone. Barker and Freddy let go of Everett and Moby dropped the gun beside him on the pillow and everyone stood there, staring at the bed. Everett was making a sound through his nose, like when he had one of his hilarious snorting fits, except the noise he was making wasn't laughter.

There was a rustle at the door, and C.P. turned to see something incredible, an actual real alien, waiting in the threshold with its hand clutching the doorknob to hold up its body. The alien was bald and had no eyebrows on its face, which squinted into the sunlight coming from the window. It stood there fighting for breath. You could see its body through the white gown it was wearing, a skinny-looking ghost with weird patterns on its torso like a bunch of tattoos. The patterns were drawn with Magic Marker. The spookiest thing, though, was its chest, which looked like a woman's except that the right side was flat and deformed, a thick scar slanting all the way to the armpit.

"Get away from my son," Mrs. Hazelrigg said. "Get away or I swear to God I'll kill you with my bare hands."

The boys marched home together, carrying their weapons limply at their sides. They didn't look at each other, or even speak. It was getting late and the trees seemed to brighten before dusk, turning damp and coppery in the last bit of daylight, as if the day's sun were being distilled from each leaf. The boys walked slowly through the cold. The street had begun to fill up with children younger than they, three-foot-tall witches and ghouls, tiny Darth Vaders, wearing long costumes so you couldn't see their feet. The creatures drifted from house to house, gripping their plastic pumpkins with two hands.

The boys had been thinking of Everett Hazelrigg, precisely because they couldn't talk about him, but now they remembered it was Halloween and their thoughts moved elsewhere. Freddy Neubaumer, who should have been devising the perfect growl to complete his impersonation of a werewolf, was thinking instead of his very first costume, a glow-in-the-dark skeleton, and how his mother, smelling wonderfully of the leaves she'd been raking, had palmed his head gently while they waited for each door to open. Barker Beemis, who in an hour or so would dress up as his idol, Evel Knievel, was thinking about trading candy with his older sister when he was four, the Halloween before she drowned in the Chesapeake, how she'd tipped a Pixy Stix into his palm and told him it was "Martian snow," the best thing he'd ever tasted. Kevin Webster, soon to be a villainous pirate, was thinking about the year he'd broken his leg a week before Halloween, how his father—gone now and living in California—had lifted him onto his shoulders and carried him from door to door that way, announcing to startled neighbors that they were a totem pole. Moby Florence, who'd convinced his parents last week to spend thirty dollars on a Satanic Avenger mask, was thinking about the homemade tiger outfit his mother had sewn for him when he was too young to distrust her taste, a costume he'd refused to take off after trick-or-treating and had worn to bed with the striped hood still warming his head.

And C. P. Pitts, already at the back of the formation and too sick at heart to care about trick-or-treating, was thinking about his own first costume—a bloodsucking vampire—which his mother had actually bought for him in advance. She'd given him plastic fangs to wear that made him lisp, dressing him in a black cape and painting his face white as Dracula's, pretending not to recognize him when she finished, saying, *Oh my God, where's C.P.? Where is he? Did you suck his blood?* backing away when he stood up as if she was a terrified woman afraid of getting her neck sucked, until finally C.P. started to get scared himself, rushing toward his mother with his arms out but it only made her shriek in horror and shrink away from his hands, cowering against the wall, until he yelled through the fangs that it was him—his name gone strange and terrible in his mouth—wanting to smear the paint from his face and show her who he was. The boys walked on, shivering in their T-shirts. They stayed together until they got to Wendover Road. Then, one by one, they branched off and headed for the warmth of their own homes, where they planned to wait until dark before reemerging as startling things: animals, or monsters, or men.

Diablo

OFELIO CAMPOS STOOD AT THE edge of the eleventh floor, dreaming of beds. He thought of showroom floors and king-size mattresses. He thought of sultanish water beds spotted like leopards. He thought of freshly washed sheets, crisp from the dryer, of a comforter he'd once slept under in a Las Vegas motel, folding him in like the wings of a bird.

Yawning, he looked through the empty window frame near his feet, peering down at the dump truck parked eleven floors below. The height made Ofelio's head swim. He held the piece of Sheetrock in his hands, nervously, trying to factor the persistent breeze into his throw. Every two weeks the construction crew finished a floor of the building and ascended to the next one, leaving a wake of rubble for him to remove. Ofelio pictured the crew like souls in purgatory, completing their penance so they could rise to the next level and labor upward. At first, on the lower floors, he'd had to heave the rubble as hard as he could just to reach his target. Now, if Ofelio exerted any strength at all, whatever he was throwing flew too far and overshot its mark, exploding against the back wall of the dump trailer. It was impossible work, like trying to thread a needle in boxing gloves. The breeze made it especially difficult. Strips of drywall strayed from their target and broke over the side of the trailer into a million pieces.

Ofelio's muscles ached, a dull pain radiating from his shoulders and throbbing downward through his limbs. He closed his eyes for a second and dreamed of leaping from the window, of drifting soundlessly through the air—a weightless slumber—before landing in the dump truck among the studs and debris. What did he care about meeting God? The *cabrón* had done him no favors. Ofelio would sleep there in his bed of rubble, a lost soul, while the crew toiled upward.

He hadn't had a good night's sleep for years. Five, six hours at the most. In letters, describing America to his family, he said: *They have the most beautiful beds in the world, but they never use them.*

Ofelio gripped the large piece of Sheetrock in his hands and held it carefully over the edge. He aimed it at the truck bed, nudging gently to the left to compensate for the breeze. The Sheetrock fell through the air without spinning. For a moment, it seemed like a perfect shot. But then it drifted from its mark and landed with a loud smack on the top of the cab, breaking into smoky fragments and making a large crater in the roof. He squeezed his eyes shut again, but it didn't undo the damage. From where he stood, the white pieces remaining on the cab looked like an unfinished jigsaw puzzle.

"Fuck!" yelled Mr. Kitchens, who'd joined Ofelio at the edge of the window frame. "Can't you aim worth shit?"

"I aimed, but the wind steal it."

"That's an International, Campos! Not a fucking Tonka toy!"

"The truck is very small. Look. Maybe this is not the intelligent way to remove trash."

"Intelligent way. Do you have any idea what that truck costs?"

Ofelio shook his head.

"You could work the rest of your life for me," Mr. Kitchens said sternly, "and not earn enough for that truck." This sounded, to Ofelio, like a profound truth. Mr. Kitchens took off his hard hat and spat into the rubble at his feet. His face was perpetually sunburned, so that the blondness of his mustache seemed strange and out of place, like something blown onto his lip. "I'll tell you something intelligent, Campos. Watching you work is like watching a monkey fuck a football."

Ofelio followed Mr. Kitchens to the freight elevator, supposing that he was meant to accompany him. He'd lived here three years already, but Mr. Kitchens's English still managed to surprise him. If his boss wasn't yelling at the crew, he was talking about Wife's Pussy. "Wife's Pussy tastes like banana cream pie," he'd say at lunch. Or: "I'll tell you something about fresh. Wife's Pussy has no preservatives. None of this Cool Whip shit." Or: "I didn't think Wife's Pussy could get any fresher, but last night she topped it all. Like sorbet, right? I was going down there to clean my palate." In Mexico, of course, there was much talk about pussies, but people would never discuss their wives' unless they were medically concerned about something. Once, in downtown San Francisco, Ofelio had run into his boss by accident; he'd been walking down the sidewalk with a large woman in a Rolling Stones T-shirt, who was scolding him in a teacherly voice. Something in Mr. Kitchens's face—a quaint and boyish misery—told Ofelio not to announce his presence.

Ofelio stepped outside into the bulldozed lot, still trailing Mr. Kitchens. With a feeling of helplessness, he rounded the hood of the dump truck to see for himself: a large fern of cracks spanned the entire width of the windshield. Mr. Kitchens sighed theatrically, as if to control his temper. "Take the rest of the day off, Campos," he said, glancing at his watch. "Try out for the Giants with that aim of yours. If you don't make the team, we'll see you tomorrow."

The construction site was in Alameda, an hour and a half by bus and BART from his apartment in the Mission District, which meant getting up at four-thirty in the morning so he could be on the train before dawn. The commute was bad enough, but he never seemed to make enough money to relax. Of the eighteen hundred dollars he earned every month, Ofelio sent nine hundred home to his wife and two children in Oaxaca. The wire transfers allowed them to pay the mortgage on their house, which he'd bought before his business—a transmission repair shop—had gone bankrupt and saddled him with debts. He was sending his son to English and computer classes at a private school there, which cost thirty dollars a week. Then there was his broke and aging father, whose farm hadn't earned a profit in six years and who refused to take money from the *técnicos* who asked him to lie about his acreage so they could steal half the subsidy themselves. And other, less urgent expenses: he couldn't resist buying American clothes for Nubia, knowing how fashionable they made her in Mexico, and he'd finally yielded to his son's tireless pleading and sent him a PlayStation 2 for Christmas. The rest of Ofelio's wages, what there were of them, went to rent and food and general necessities, whatever it took to get him from one day to the next.

He didn't blame his family about the gifts, of course: he'd felt the same way about American things before coming here, as if his life—his hopes and dreams and successes—were somehow inferior without them. He'd come here originally to pay off his debts, so he wouldn't end up like his father, but also to relieve this sense of geographical misfortune.

Ofelio climbed the steps to his apartment, the smell of urine stinging his nostrils. His legs felt weak and waterlogged, as if he were trying to surface from the bottom of a lake. On his way to the fourth floor he passed the apartment below his, whose entrance was knotted with people speaking clamorously in Chinese. The people were holding drinks and paper plates wilting with grease. They lifted their plates to let him pass. Upstairs in his apartment, Ofelio's brother was lying in his boxer shorts on the foldout couch, watching an American talk show on TV.

"You're home early," he said in Spanish, surprised.

"I took the afternoon off."

"Loafer," his brother said, plumping the pillows behind his head. "You're lucky I'm not entertaining a woman friend." Adolfo worked the night shift as a janitor at a law office, which meant he slept much of the day until Ofelio came home. The different schedules made sharing a studio apartment bearable.

"They're having another party downstairs," Ofelio said, collapsing into a mildewy chair in the corner. "That's the third one this week."

"Maybe it's a Chinese holiday." Adolfo put a finger on each temple and stretched the corners of his eyes, so that he looked like a squirrel.

"Last night she was singing in the middle of the night. The lady from downstairs. The tiny one? Singing at the top of her lungs." He'd have to discuss the singing with the lady's husband, a small, nervous-looking man with one ear shriveled into his head, like the coin slot in a vending machine. He saw the man all the time but had never spoken to him. Chinese people, with their fishy breath, made him sick to his stomach.

On TV, a woman with a microphone was interviewing policemen who'd posed for a sexy calendar. The policemen were wearing T-shirts that said OFFICER HUNK. When one of them stood up and took off his shirt, the audience of women hooted and pounded their feet. Ofelio asked his brother how he could watch such crap.

"It's very informative. I'm learning about law enforcement." Adolfo glanced at his own chest, which was flat and hairless. "Actually, I'm thinking about changing careers."

Ofelio managed a laugh. "You want to be a policeman?"

"There are many perks to this job." He gestured at the hooting women.

"I'd like to see you show up to police school without your papers." Ofelio suppressed a yawn, eyes blurring with tears. "Besides, if you were a cop, you'd have to deport me. I heard it on the radio: they just passed a law so that normal police can arrest us like la Migra. They've already started in New York."

"You're a great pessimist, Ofelio. This is America. Everything's possible. You want me to be cleaning toilets the rest of my life." Adolfo insisted he could be a policeman—it was just a matter of finding an American wife.

"My brother," Ofelio said gently. "You will never find an American wife with your hair like that. You look like a porn star."

He touched the back of his hair, which was shaved neatly on the sides but fell into a thick mane down his back. "What do *you* know? You're just visiting, right?"

Ofelio stared at the TV, ignoring his brother's sarcasm. He knew that everybody said they were returning to Mexico, if not immediately then in a year or two, and that most of them—except for the *braceros,* who spent their lives floating back and forth—never did. But Ofelio was different. He didn't—like his brother, for example—try to live as an American on *mojado* wages. He never went out to eat and spent nearly every evening at home, except for two nights a week when he attended free classes at City College to sharpen his English. These past three years, working overtime until his feet bled, he hadn't even bought himself a new pair of boots. And the frugality had served him: he'd managed to pay off his debts, one week at a time. If he saved five thousand dollars, he could return home and have enough money to keep his son in school for the next year, maybe even buy a piece of land near his father's. That was his dream: to start his own ranch. It wasn't so much, five thousand. The trick was, always, to remember his real life was elsewhere.

"Which reminds me," Adolfo said now, pointing at the picture of Nubia framed prominently on the windowsill. "If your beautiful wife won't clean up after herself, I'm going to start charging her rent."

Ofelio blushed. In front of the picture was an open can of Coke and a single, untouched tamale resting on a plate. Every Sunday, Ofelio would buy tamales from the Mexican grocery and sit beside his wife's photograph, pretending they were having dinner together—just as Nubia would set a place for him, extravagantly, at home. It was something they'd agreed to before he left. They'd never said it in so many words, but Ofelio knew it was a vow of some kind, a symbol of their not having dinner with anyone else.

A commercial came on TV for a store selling Posturepedic mattresses. In the commercial, a crowd of insomniacs in pajamas were walking in a zombielike mass through the streets and funneling into the entrance of the store, which glowed with a celestial light. The store was called Sleepland.

"Everything okay, brother?" Adolfo asked, eyeing him strangely.

"I need to lie down, I think."

Ofelio got up slowly and clunked across the room in his

work boots and opened the door to the closet, which doubled as his sleeping quarters. The light flickered on after a few seconds. He had to stand on the mattress in order to shut the door, balancing on the saggy edge where he'd sawed the mattress up the middle in order to fit it into the closet. Generally he slept on the foldout couch, unless Adolfo wasn't working and needed it himself. The arrangement had been fine at first, but for the past month they'd cut back Adolfo's hours at work, and Ofelio was sleeping in the closet four nights a week.

Ofelio sat on the mattress with his clothes on, keeping the light on for a minute in order to set his alarm clock. It was only five-fifteen, but he was planning to sleep through the night. As was his custom before bed, he reached into the corner of the closet and lifted the papier-mâché devil at his feet, weighing it carefully in his hands. His son had sent the two-foot doll with blue horns to him last March, meaning for him to destroy it on Semana Santa, to blow it up with a firecracker as they did at home. Ofelio was using it as a piggy bank. He'd pierced a small hole between its legs where he could thread a hundred-dollar bill rolled like a cigarette. It was something his brother would get a kick out of, that he was sticking his earnings up the devil's ass. But it was his private savings, and he hadn't told even Adolfo about it.

Tonight, as always, the devil seemed to mock him, smirking at him from a *bandido* mustache and green polka-dotted face. *Buey*, it said, *you will never save enough money.*

Yes, I will. I've put two thousand in your ass already.

Ha! Try one thousand. That sounds more accurate.

I've been counting. You can't fool me, cabrón.

It's my ass. I should know what goes up it. Besides, do I feel any heavier?

Ofelio had to admit the devil did not feel heavier. He put it back in the corner and yanked off the light and lay stiffly in the dark. His muscles burned so much from heaving Sheetrock that he thought he might actually split into pieces, crack open like papier-mâché. Sometimes it was hard to separate the actual pain in his body from the pangs of longing he felt for his family. It was deeply physical, this longing. Thoughts of Nubia, in particular, made Ofelio's body hurt: the simple image of her neck, smooth as the girdled part of a tree when she lifted her hair, could keep him awake for hours. Touching himself helped, but often Ofelio's arms ached too much even to do that.

And then there were the other women, the ones he saw every day waiting for the train or talking to handsome men in restaurants or striding purposefully down the street with their eyes glued to the sidewalk. They were everywhere, stirring Ofelio's thoughts and clouding him with desire. At night, he'd imagine his wife above him and she would turn into someone else, a stranger he'd noticed on the street, some tall-booted woman that might slake his loneliness. Afterward, cleaning himself with a T-shirt, he'd feel stained and miserable, scented with betrayal.

Adolfo's talk show had changed to something else, a toneless murmur jarred by a laugh track. Downstairs the festivities continued: Chinese laughter, pots clanking in the sink. Ofelio lay there for a long time, listening to the racket below him. In a little while, the city's lovers would steal off to their huge and beautiful beds, hugging each other to sleep if they were too wiped out to make love. Ofelio's throat felt parched. He realized that he couldn't bear another night in the closet. This was death, the dark constriction of a coffin. He opened the door and squeezed back into the room, plucking his coat from the chair.

"I've got to get out of this apartment. Let's get a beer somewhere."

Adolfo regarded him in astonishment. "Who are you? Is this

1365 York Street? Where's Ofelio, my cheapskate brother who doesn't drink?"

"Still there," he said, gesturing at the closet. "Asleep."

Adolfo took him to a place on Bryant Street, a gringo bar he'd started frequenting in hopes of finding a wife. Ofelio looked around, taking note of the shiny new booths filled with young people dressed in disheveled, mismatched clothes. The walls were painted with stars and planets and flaming comets that seemed to be raining apocalyptically on the poorly dressed customers while they sipped their drinks. Ofelio was starting to have second thoughts about coming out, though he was glad he hadn't bothered to gel his hair. At the rear of the bar, across from the pool table, was a small stage with a single microphone centered in front of a stool.

"What is this '*neat-A*'?" Adolfo asked the bartender. He pointed at a banner over the stage that said OPEN MIKE NITE. Adolfo, though he'd been here for five years, spoke far less English than Ofelio.

"You mean 'night,'" the bartender said, laughing. "It's open mike tonight, which means anyone can perform. Fifteen minutes of fame."

Adolfo nodded, unwedging the slice of lime from his Corona. "These gringos can't spell their own language," he said in Spanish when the bartender had left.

The man sitting next to Adolfo started to tell a joke, entertaining two women who were standing at the bar with expressions of tolerant misgiving. The man was older than the other customers and had a short beard that he'd forked into two prongs with rubber bands. The joke was about an old lady who's magically granted three wishes. On her last wish, she asks that her poodle be transformed into an eighteen-year-old bodybuilder. "So that night she asks to see his pecker," the man said drunkenly, "but then the guy drops his pants and says"—he switched to a high-pitched voice—"'Bet you're sorry you had me neutered!'" When the two women failed to laugh, the man looked at Adolfo and Ofelio.

"What means 'pecker'?" Adolfo asked, smiling.

"You know," the man said, leaning toward him. "Cock. Schlong. I was being polite for the women." He looked at Ofelio helplessly and then pointed at Adolfo's crotch. "Peee-nuus," he said loudly.

Adolfo scowled. Someone called a name from the pool table in the back and the man got up, lurching from his stool. The two women said something to each other in private, glancing in the direction of the pool table before bursting into laughter. Adolfo stood up gallantly so the women could sit together. They tried to decline, but he insisted, grinning in a way that concealed his silver tooth. Ofelio was embarrassed by his brother's chivalry; the feeling shamed him, because he knew he wouldn't be embarrassed if the women were Latina.

The taller woman, a fair-skinned blond with freckles crowding her face, set her glass on the bar in order to shake their hands. "Alden," she said, "like the pond, but without the 'W.'" She frowned, glancing from Adolfo to Ofelio and back again. She introduced her friend, whose face was puffed into a grimace. The woman bowed her head, trying to smile through the paralysis of her lips. It was the first time Ofelio had ever seen a gringa blush in his presence.

"Gum surgery," Alden explained. "She didn't want to come out tonight, but I dragged her anyway."

The woman—Chloe was her name—hid her mouth with a napkin and tried to speak, but her voice sounded like a cassette tape after being warped by the sun. Ofelio couldn't make out a word she was saying. Alden urged her to show them what she really looked like, and Chloe took a photograph from her purse and passed it to Adolfo for them to see. The picture showed an attractive woman in dark glasses standing next to a tremendous tree trunk.

"Sister?" Adolfo asked.

"Mnuhhhh," Chloe said. She pointed at herself, lifting a lock of her hair. Adolfo handed the picture back with a serious look, within which Ofelio guessed was the first minor cue of seduction.

"You too much more pretty than sister," he said.

The woman glanced at her friend in distress. Adolfo, perhaps relieved to be talking to someone whose English was worse than his, started to tell her about their own sister—a housekeeper in Salina Cruz—in half-mimed sentences. For his own part, Ofelio wasn't accustomed to drinking beer and found himself striking up a conversation with the freckled woman named Alden, who seemed impressed by his English. He told her about the classes he was taking at City College, how they spent an hour every Tuesday reading a book about successful immigrants.

"It's called *Sí, Se Puede,*" he said. "We talk about famous people. César Chávez. Carlos Santana. We are supposed to be confident and follow our dream."

"Maybe I should take that class," she said, frowning. She told him that she was hoping to go to design school next fall but worked at a beauty store to pay the rent, selling expensive soap to tourists. She reached into her coat pocket and handed him a ball of soap, a brown sphere that looked suspiciously like a turd. He couldn't imagine anyone wanting to wash with it. "Keep it. The distributor came by today and left a bunch of free samples."

Ofelio put the soap in the pocket of his own jacket. Alden studied his face for a second and then asked him where he was from, ducking her head forward to listen.

"Oh, God," she said. "I love Oaxaca. I went there . . . what? Two years ago? The Night of the Radishes. And those little black animals—what do you call them?" She looked at him again and seemed suddenly embarrassed. "You probably wonder why we go nuts for this stuff. Crafts, I mean."

"Yes," he admitted. He supposed, in some way, it was related to his son's wanting a PlayStation 2. "I don't really care about these things." He told her how the rug sellers in Oaxaca bought carpets from small towns near his father's ranch and then sold them for ten times the price. Very hard to make an honest living in the city. Before he could stop himself, he was telling her about his own failed business, the stranglehold of his debts, how he'd left Mexico when his wife was pregnant and had never even seen his two-year-old daughter in person.

"Why doesn't your family come here?"

"It's very expensive. Also dangerous."

"That's terrible." Alden stared at her drink, a delta of concern denting her forehead. "Oaxaca's so beautiful. You must think about it every day."

"Yes," he lied. In fact, he found himself thinking less and less of it, which alarmed him. The handsome buildings, the stray dogs in the *zócalo*, the sun like a weight on his face—he had to think now to remember them. It was one reason he was desperate to get home. And, of course, there were the things he felt guilty about not missing: the lines at the bank, say, or how when he bought flowers for Nubia, walking back to their house, *machos* used to taunt him from their cars and call him *mariposa*.

Alden asked him what it was he thought about most.

"My wife. Of course."

She smiled. "What's she like?"

"She is beautiful, but in a Mexican way. She loves food and is *un poco gordita*. A little unskinny? She's very smart too— when I had the business, she did all the accounts herself and saw over the customers. We are the perfect match." He glanced at Alden, ashamed at this idealized portrait of his marriage. "Of course, we argue too. Sometimes she is jealous. Before I left for America, she became very upset. She sees the TV from the United States, you know, where every woman is thin. She yelled at me and says that I'll fall in love with a skinny American."

Alden closed her eyes for a few seconds, as if she were trying to memorize a phone number. Ofelio realized for the first time that she was drunk. He couldn't help noticing, despite the dim light of the bar, that even her eyelids had freckles on them.

"It must be very lonely without your family," she said, touching his arm.

Instinctively, Ofelio glanced over at his brother, surprised to discover that his stool was empty. He scanned the booths along the wall before finding him near the pool table, waiting by the chalkboard and showing Chloe how to hold a cue. A woman with a tattoo on her biceps and red streaks in her hair mounted the small stage across from them and sat in front of the microphone. The bar fell silent. She said she would read something she'd written, a poem called "Untitled: Prayer to Myself." *If only you would speak,* it began. The woman kept her head down while she read and refused to look at the audience, staring at her lap in a bout of shyness. Ofelio listened carefully but didn't understand what the poem meant, only that the woman kept repeating the word "savior." After a while, he realized that she wasn't bowing her head from shyness at all: rather, she seemed to be addressing her own sexual organ, beseeching it in a progressively louder voice.

> *Deliver me from soap operas, from Doritos, from*
> *Walgreens in the afternoon.*
> *You are the throb of a hummingbird's wings.*
> *Wonderful savior! Pleasure! Float me to the sun.*

The audience of customers clapped politely, waiting for the woman to climb off the stage. Americans seemed to be obsessed with genitalia. The depth of Ofelio's exhaustion, coupled with the two Coronas he'd drunk, was making him feel a bit unsteady, as if he were perched atop a ledge.

"I should bring my boss here to say a lecture," he said over the applause.

Alden cupped her ear as if she'd heard him incorrectly. The bar grew quiet for the next reader, a man with a green patch under his lip like a slick of algae. Alden cocked her head while the man read into the microphone. Her hair grazed Ofelio's arm, which was resting on the bar. Ofelio tried to focus on what was being said, hoping to learn some new words, but all he could think about was the feathery touch of her hair.

"My ex-boyfriend writes poetry," she said during the intermission. "Thierry, his name is. I just call him 'asshole.' Sometimes he'll fast—not eat anything—for a whole week."

"Why?" Ofelio asked.

"To clear his thoughts. Like if he has an important decision to make."

"You mean like where to go to dinner?" he joked.

"No. God." She laughed. "It does seem kind of crazy, doesn't it?"

Crossing the border, Ofelio had spent three days in a motel room with fourteen other people and no food. He'd felt as if he might die. "Where is he now? This asshole?"

Alden looked down at her drink. "He dumped me. Three weeks ago. Fell in love with a woman from his yoga class. Hence the 'asshole.'" She lifted her glass in mock salute, a napkin clinging like a leaf to the bottom. "Actually, there are a lot of names. That's just the most versatile."

Ofelio reached over to remove the napkin from her glass and accidentally skimmed the front of her sweater. He yanked his hand back as their eyes met, a lingering glance. I should go home, he thought. As he rose from his stool, a commotion broke out in the rear of the bar. He stood on his toes to get a better look and saw two men locked in an ardent struggle behind the pool table. The men were yelling, knocking into things as they fought. It took Ofelio a minute to recognize Adolfo: he was being overwhelmed by the man with the forked beard, shoved backward against the cue rack.

Drunkenly, Ofelio rushed across the bar and bumped through a crowd of bystanders, grabbing the hulking man by the back of his shirt and trying to pull him off his brother. The man turned. Ofelio didn't see the punch so much as sense it, a psychic flash that sent him toppling against the jukebox. The world darkened and then returned, glittering in tiny specks. A rain of sequins. He'd never seen snow before but imagined it would look as beautiful as this. He tried to focus his eyes, but only one of them seemed to work. The bass from the jukebox shuddered through his body. Eventually, someone helped him to his feet and steadied him against the wall before walking him toward the door. He couldn't follow what happened next except that they were sitting on the curb, he and Alden and Adolfo, the blindness in his eye opening to a bright and painful sliver.

Adolfo lit a cigarette and began smoking it in tiny puffs. His T-shirt was torn at the neck, hanging down like the flap of a tent. Otherwise, he seemed unscathed.

"What happened?" Ofelio asked. The world had stopped snowing, but his head felt damp and woolly.

"Fucking crazy gringo," Adolfo said in Spanish. "It was my turn to play pool. He said to stand back, because he was going to mop the floor with me. I understand 'mop'—but why the hell does he want to do it together? I asked if he was the janitor of the bar, which is when he attacked me." He laughed and clapped Ofelio's shoulder. "Luckily, Ofelio Tyson stopped by to teach him a lesson."

"Where's Chloe?" Alden asked.

"*Se fue.* Mouth problem. No happy." He grinned at Ofelio. "I'd like to meet her sister," he said suggestively, slipping back into Spanish. He felt Ofelio's biceps with one hand and then raised his fists in a pugilistic stance. Crouched there behind his scrawny arms, he looked like a happy teenager. Adolfo checked his watch and bowed graciously at Alden before running off to work with his hair bobbing behind him, punching the air with his fists.

It struck Ofelio, suddenly, that his brother was in despair— had been for many years. Alden leaned forward and examined Ofelio's eye, tipping his chin back to catch the light of the arc lamp. He could smell the sweat on her skin mingled with perfume. It was a damp earth smell, sweet and unpleasant at the same time.

"That's a real beauty. Better let me get some ice on it."

Ofelio stumbled back to his apartment, his head groggy from the stranger's punch. He had trouble opening the door, and Alden helped him fit the key into the lock. The place was a mess, dirty clothes thrown into a makeshift pile in the corner. He'd left the door to the closet open, and you could see the sawed-off mattress blocking the threshold. He wasn't embarrassed. It was his life. Not the one he would have chosen, but a life nonetheless.

Alden told him to lie on the foldout couch and then rummaged through the refrigerator and reappeared with something in her hand, a dish towel filled with foul-smelling ice. He would let her take care of him. He would allow this to happen— because his eye hurt and he was drunk and he liked the way she smelled—and then he would ask her to leave. Alden knelt beside him. He closed his eye and she nursed it with the towel, pressing gently until his face felt strange and conspicuous, a faint ache clutching his forehead.

"This should help the swelling," she said into his ear. Her voice was low and slurred. She glanced around the tiny studio, eyes sweeping the room before snagging on the windowsill, studying the picture behind the Coke can and uneaten tamale.

"What's your wife's name?"

"Nubia."

"That's very pretty. Pretend I'm Nubia."

Something in Ofelio's heart chinked open, like a door. He closed his good eye as well, picturing his wife's face as she spoke to him. He liked that she had a gringa's voice, strange and untunable. He reached for her with his eyes closed. *Maybe we shouldn't,* the voice said, but he didn't listen, amazed at the boniness of her hips.

Ofelio woke to the sound of singing from downstairs. Chinese opera. He tried to sleep but the singing continued, clawing through his ear and raking at his nerves. His eye throbbed in the dark. The noise went on for so long he thought he might actually cry. In a desperate fantasy, he imagined strangling the tiny woman with his bare hands, savoring the quiet as she slackened in his grip. Finally he got up and grabbed a broom from its place in the corner.

"*¡Cállate!*" He banged on the floor with the heel of the broom. The glass doors to the cupboards rattled in the kitchen. "Shut up!" he screamed in English. "You can't sing! Go back to China, you stupid-eye witch!"

The singing stopped. He turned, suddenly ashamed. Alden was sitting up in bed, her body white enough to locate in the dark. She mumbled something he didn't understand before lying back down and cocooning herself under the covers. Ofelio got back in bed and listened to the breathing next to him, the drunken rhythm so different from his wife's, too sick at heart to sleep.

The next day at work he roamed the eleventh floor in a daze, trundling wheelbarrows of debris and dumping them on the platform of the freight elevator. Clouds of dust stung the raw skin at his eyebrow. Mr. Kitchens, framing his instructions like a concession to Ofelio's ineptitude, had decided it was a better idea to lift the debris out than to hurl it eleven stories to the dump truck. "Better stop looking in your neighbor's keyhole," he said, staring at Ofelio's eye. His co-workers were equally impressed by his appearance, regarding him with a new and curious respect. They threw air punches when he passed or veered out of his way in mock fright. Ofelio ignored them, too tired to respond. He could barely lift the wheelbarrow without falling on his face. At one point he almost rolled himself right into the elevator shaft, not noticing that someone had ridden the platform down while he was away.

The crew stopped for a midmorning break, smoking around the gang box. Ofelio wiped the sweat from his eye; the morning had begun to heat up, fog lifting to reveal a smudge of sun. As he was folding up his jacket, the brown ball of soap Alden had given him fell out and rolled across the concrete.

"Jesus, Campos," one of the journeymen said, pretending to gawk. "They beat you up and shit in your pocket?"

Ofelio ignored the crew's laughter, too miserable to think of a comeback. He wondered if Alden was awake. He'd gotten up quietly, unable to face her in the light of dawn. Well, his brother would be home by now—he could bid her farewell if she wasn't gone already.

He sat by himself near a stack of wallboard, touching the puffy curve of his eyelid to gauge its swelling. He had no idea how bad it was: since he'd gotten up, wretched from thoughts of Nubia, he couldn't bear to look at himself in a mirror.

After lunch, Ofelio swung by the trailer to pick up his pay. Mr. Kitchens sat behind his desk in reading glasses, dispensing checks from a lockbox. A red mark circled his forehead, like a crown. The workers ahead of Ofelio received their checks, signing their names into a grease-stained ledger before stepping aside to rip open their envelopes. The walls of the trailer were plastered with bikini-clad women, their faces limp and slack-jawed, as if they'd been struck over the head with frying pans. Ordinarily the posters seemed like harmless wallpaper, but today they filled him with an obscure and welcome anger.

When he reached the front of the line, Mr. Kitchens counted out a stack of hundreds and handed them to him in a wad. Ofelio blinked, staring at the bills in his hand.

"Me faltan dos cientos," he said, recounting them carefully. "You owe me two hundred."

Mr. Kitchens scribbled something in the ledger. "You're lucky I'm not a tightwad. It'll cost me more than that to replace the windshield. Not to mention the cab, which I'm banging out myself." He looked Ofelio in the eye. "This isn't some orphanage we're running."

Ofelio left the trailer and stopped a yard or so from the entrance, squinting at a piece of rebar glinting in the dirt. The sun lay on his back without actually warming it. Beside the rebar, melting in a pool of colors, was a half-eaten Popsicle. From the trailer he heard Mr. Kitchens talking about Wife's Pussy, extolling its freshness by comparing it to a mountain spring. *Swear to you, boys, you could bottle her fucking piss and sell it in Paris.*

It was the voice, lewd and declamatory at the same time, that drove him. Ofelio picked up the rebar at his feet and went back inside the trailer, the heat of the metal scalding his hand. He walked through the crowd of workers, grabbed Mr. Kitchens by the shirt, and pulled him from his chair so that his sunburned face loomed close to his own. He raised the rebar like an ax. Mr. Kitchens's face seemed to have aged suddenly by thirty years, grown dumb and wide-eyed as a trout's. Flecks of gray dotted his mustache. Except for the faint wheeze of his panting, the room was silent. Ofelio closed his eyes for a second, imagining the nose shattering under his blow, the tight-lipped smile bashed into a blizzard of teeth. He could see everything perfectly. But when he opened his eyes again, all he saw was a frightened man in glasses, lips trembling under a graying mustache, closer to the face he'd seen that day when Mrs. Kitchens scolded him on the street.

Ofelio let go of his boss, who slumped back into his chair. He walked out of the trailer and across the sun-caked lot and all the way to the bus stop without looking back. The rage in his heart had disappeared, leaving only the deep and familiar weariness. On the bus, the driver studied him warily before closing the doors, observing him in the giant mirror above his head, as if Ofelio was a drunk out to make trouble. His eye twitched in a painful rhythm unconnected to his pulse. It wasn't until Ofelio had settled into a window seat near the back that he realized he was still holding the rebar. As he watched the world drift by his window—the commuters chatting on their cell phones, wearing ties or dresses or uniforms—the reality of what he'd done sank in. He'd lose his job. There was no way around it. He had seven hundred dollars in his pocket, all of which he'd have to wire to Oaxaca. There was next month's mortgage to pay off, his son's tuition. Even if he found a new job in a week, he'd lose six days' wages. The thought of spending any of the money in his closet—what he was saving for his ranch—made him utterly depressed.

He had a vision, a terrible fantasy, of the papier-mâché devil broken on the bed, Alden dashing down the street to buy herself some expensive clothes.

When he got home, Ofelio rushed upstairs and wedged open the closet. The devil was still there, leering at him from the corner while a squawk of voices rose from downstairs. Incredibly, his neighbors seemed to be having another party. Ofelio stalked down the steps in an angry fog. A Chinese couple who looked to be about his age were standing in the threshold, drinking from teacups. Through the open door, he could see some kids running around inside the apartment, chasing each other and shrieking like monkeys.

"What's happening here?" Ofelio asked the people in the doorway. "It's two-thirty in the afternoon!"

"My father-in-law," the man said gravely, in unaccented English. He held the porcelain teacup with two hands, which were veinless and perfectly manicured. They were the most beautiful hands Ofelio had ever seen. "He passed away on Tuesday. Very sudden." He tilted his head, squinting at Ofelio. "Did you know Mr. Tan?"

"No," Ofelio said, taken aback. "*Un poquito*. Only by eye. I live upstairs."

The man studied him carefully. He raised one of his beautiful hands and gripped Ofelio's arm at the shoulder.

"I can see it's a shock," he said. "Come in and have some tea with us."

Despite Ofelio's protests, the man steered him into the room, an immaculate studio with a layout identical to his brother's. For a minute, in his trancelike exhaustion, Ofelio had the disconcerting impression that he'd wandered into his own apartment. There were flowers arranged in plastic vases, a calendar on the wall with a picture of a puppy on it. Ofelio walked in slowly, wary of disturbing the gathering. He saw now that it wasn't actually a party but a handful of relatives assembled in mourning. Mrs. Tan was sitting by herself at a plastic table in the kitchen area, eyes raw from weeping. She dabbed at her face with a kitchen sponge. She was so small that her feet barely reached the ground. Ofelio's boots squeaked on the tile floor; the tiny woman looked at him, her face bright with tears. He realized he'd been mistaken those times in the middle of the night, that she must have been wailing in grief.

Ofelio bowed his head, a flush of shame heating his face. It seemed remarkable that an entire life could be lived here, that someone could grow old and die in a space no bigger than this. The man with beautiful hands led him around the couch, avoiding the children scampering through the room. On the windowsill, arranged like an altar, was a framed picture of Mr. Tan. The photo had been taken from a clever angle, so you couldn't see the shriveled slot of the man's ear. Ofelio felt something—a coldness—slink across his scalp. Crowding the picture, among other offerings, was an open can of Coke and a plate laden with gluey white buns.

He let the man with beautiful hands lead him past the window and ease him into a chair.

The next week Ofelio tried to find a job, hunting around at construction sites he'd heard about from his former co-workers, taking buses all the way to Alameda or San Leandro or Mill Valley before discovering they didn't need him. The economy was bust: why hire *illegales* when they could get gringos for the same rate? Eventually he gave up looking for construction work and tried to get a job like his brother's, cleaning toilets or washing dishes. He combed the newspaper for openings, impatiently, but couldn't find a thing.

After a few weeks he took the papier-mâché devil from his closet and smashed it open on the floor of the apartment. Two thousand bucks, as he'd thought. Seeing the shattered doll like that, headless and forlorn, gave him a grim sort of pleasure. He stuck half the money under his mattress for reserve. After allotting five hundred for his family, he went to a store on Mission Street and bought himself a new pair of boots, walking the aisles to make sure they were comfortable. The salesclerk steered him toward a shirt, a plaid flannel with a handsome cut. Ofelio liked the colors. Paying for the clothes at the cashier counter, he felt an odd lifting in his heart, as if someone had forgiven him a debt.

Adolfo came home the next morning and saw the shards of devil scattered on the floor. He foraged a blue horn from the corner. Ever since discovering Alden in his bed, he'd looked at Ofelio differently, like a boy who'd seen through a magician's trick. "I work all night cleaning floors, and what happens?"

"I'll pick it up," Ofelio said. "Get off my back."

Adolfo turned away, disgusted. "I don't mind sweeping out your women, but you'll have to clean up after your fights."

That night Ofelio called his family, who were waiting by the phone. His daughter was learning the noises for animals and made a sound like a sheep. Ofelio did his best to laugh. He tried talking to his wife, but the careless affection in her voice made him queasy and he had to get off.

Of course, he hadn't told his family about attacking Mr. Kitchens and losing his job, or that he'd started going down to Cesar Chavez Street every morning, waiting for work with the other day laborers. The laborers had made him take a vow, ensuring he wouldn't work for less than ten dollars an hour. It didn't seem to make much sense, given the number of people lining the sidewalk. On the rare occasion when a car pulled up, they raced each other to the curb and smothered it from all sides, whistling through their teeth. More often than not, no one picked Ofelio up and he'd stand there all morning with the sun baking his face, staring at the bank of fog receding from the hills of Twin Peaks.

Some of the laborers had been in the city only a week or so, arriving here from places like Conchagua or Zacatecas or Guatemala City. Ofelio found himself helping the new arrivees with their English. He taught them words, sounding each one carefully while they watched his lips.

Sky. Shoelace. Apart.

One morning, sitting against the wall of a karate studio, he saw Alden and her friend crossing the street on their way from Precita Park. They were laughing about something, their heads pitched back at the same angle. Ofelio hid his face and didn't wave.

Later, a red pickup slowed in front of him and stopped a little way down the curb, but he let the other laborers run after it and didn't get up. It felt too nice to sit. Rent was due in a few days, but he still had plenty of money—he'd stopped counting a while ago, since delving into the bills under his mattress. He used to sit like this as a boy sometimes, leaning against the wall of their ranch house when he was supposed to be shucking corn for dinner, making Adolfo do all the work while he drifted off to sleep. The men shouted at him from the bed of the pickup. He was half asleep already, lost to the drowsy orbit of his thoughts. He remembered that day in the Chinese woman's apartment—how exhausted he'd been, as if his head was packed in clay, and how the man with beautiful hands had guided him to a chair, mistaking him for a mourner. He could feel the hand now, pressing his shoulder. "Make yourself at home," the man had said, and Ofelio had all but forgotten who he was, such a relief it seemed to rest.

Neon Tetra

TWO WORDS, SIMPLE YET AMAZING in their pairing—"neon" wrested from its natural successor "sign," "tetra" mysterious in a way he could only guess at, like the name of a galaxy or a female superhero with silver boots—and yet his father used them so plainly, the commonest of words, as if he were describing something missing from the fridge, grapefruit juice or the gas can of maple syrup from Vermont or his imported German horseradish: *What we need's some neon tetras,* a need the boy hadn't even known they'd had, but of course they did, he felt it like a leak in his heart as soon as he heard the words, a way to express the blundering need he felt when he lurked behind his father for no reason, trailing him from room to room or bugging him when he was trying to read his *Hemmings Motor News* (his father, exasperated, dropping the magazine and saying, "What do you *need,* son?"), asking his father to chuck the baseball around the yard or fix the transformer for the Marklin train set in the cellar that he knew how to fix himself, and yet the need was still there, even after he smelled his father's Coke-breath beside him and the transformer was wired up properly and the train began its loop through a parched and peopleless world, the cars flickering past deserted depots and trees the size of broccoli stalks and gas stations adrift from roads or customers, a landscape like a figuration of the boy's own loneliness.

Neon tetra. The boy said the words to himself as they drove toward the tropical pet store, which they'd been visiting all summer to buy fish, his father's interest having moved from model trains to a casket-long fish tank in the living room. He tried to conjure a fish as beautiful as the name, imagining—despite his wish to be sensible—one shaped like a naked woman, a miniature mermaid, smooth and flawless and unfathomable as his sister's only Barbie doll, which the boy undressed every day before she got home from field hockey, removing the tiny socks and unsnapping the skirt and mysterious shirt-sweater she groomed with a Monopoly iron, unappeased when he was finished with nothing left to remove and no words to describe the plastic lightness of its body. How different it was from the naked bodies he saw in the book in the TV room, the one called *The Tribes of Africa,* with the pictures of women cracking from their skins like dropped Easter eggs, their breasts hanging enormously, incredibly to their stomachs, baffling him with their strangeness, until he'd asked his mother if only black women had nipples and the blush of her face—its shy deflection of his question—had confirmed his suspicion.

The streets changed as his father drove in the direction of downtown, past the 7-Eleven that was as far as the boy ever ventured on his bike, leaving behind the quiet shade of their own neighborhood, the pin oaks and badminton nets drooping into grins and men with garden hoses tossing lassos of water on the grass (each man mincing through a lawn of toys, Big Wheels and lacrosse sticks and Nerf footballs chewed into abstract rocks of coral)—thrillingly, all that disappearing now as they turned into the streets of downtown Baltimore, into a block of close-together houses and graffiti on the sidewalks and cars with newspaper replacing one window. Slowly, rolling their own windows to a crack despite the heat, they drove past fenced-in yards no bigger than the pen where his father kept his hunting dogs, people sweating on their stoops or blowing up inflatable pools on their laps or pulling oxygen tanks down the sidewalk in a prayerful trance. The boy knew nothing about these people, only that they haunted homes in his own neighborhood in the middle of the night, leaving traces of their presence: vanished speakers or mud smears on the rug or sofas glittering with glass. But he loved the downtown glare and swelter, because it made the inside of the fish store seem all the more remarkable, the lavender hush that felt like a rescue, absorbing you in its glow, urging you downstairs to the pretty girl who worked the counter, a girl (named strangely as the fish) who was black but wore T-shirts with fancy beads sewn on them so the boy couldn't see if she had nipples, who smelled nicely of perfume—like the center of a leaf pile, rich and nutmegy and pleasant—and would take him to the back of the store at his father's request, leading them past the turtles and geckos and giant toads into the burbling catacombs of fish.

Here we are, his father said now, pulling into the parking lot with a cautious bump and edging the Buick past the open spaces along the graffitied wall of the store, past the words DALE'S TROPIC WORLD and the big angelfish muraled beneath them—an ethereal, spray-painted penis dangling like a worm above its mouth—turning the corner until they were behind the building where the Dumpster was, his father choosing this particular spot to park the Buick though there were no other cars in the lot. He seemed excited (neon tetra!) but also vaguely uncomfortable, a feeling the boy traced to the sunburn on his father's legs, which were covered now by khakis but had looked miraculous yesterday as his father sunbathed by the pool in his swim trunks, an event that had shocked the boy and his mother both, considering that his fair-skinned father never wore shorts even to the beach: but there he was, half naked on the deck— so white he looked incomplete, like a half-crayoned figure in a coloring book—surprising them as they walked to the back door of the house, the surprise fading into a quiet amazement until the boy's mother had turned and said in a voice as thin as her face: *Look at the bathing beauty!* And now, cutting the engine of the Buick, his father did something equally astonishing, squeaking the rearview mirror with his hand until he could see himself in the glass and then unbuttoning the second button of his shirt so that a gleam of burn was revealed, a perfect triangle of red, a few pale hairs sprouting over the V of his shirt and curling along the placket.

He opened the door finally, and the boy followed him around the front of the lot into the store itself, descending into the gentle, humming world of tanks, the audible glow that made it seem as if you were underwater as well, his father leading him past the counter and adjacent rack hung with bags of Technicolor pebbles, wandering down the row of lizards and newts and puddled toads before finding a man the boy had never seen before, a chubby guy with little moles clustered on one cheek. They stopped beside him, waiting as the man scooped something from a tank—a dead eel, doodled in his net—until his father asked where Kaswana was and the man told him she was sick, home all day while he had to miss the Orioles game, twenty-dollar tickets he couldn't even scalp, and his father stood there with a weird smile on his lips and asked him if she were running a fever, the man saying, *Beats me, mis-*

ter, she wasn't giving me the play-by-play. The boy's father looked down at his lap and then seemed to glance around the store for the first time, his face losing its brightness and taking on a customary distracted gloom, even a tinge of anger, and he turned to the man inspecting the tank to say, *The boy wants some neon tetras,* as if it was the boy's own idea and his father were just bending to a whim. They followed the chubby man without pausing to linger over the catfish or oscars or stingrays like steamrolled sharks (which was what the boy loved about coming here, the sense of rare lingering, his father talking to the nice-smelling girl at the counter until she had to close up the store), passing the litany of names, all the wonderful word pairs he couldn't match with specific fish, ruby scat and yellow tang and the nightmarishly named clown knife, his father not so much as glancing at the tanks and the boy remembering the other hobbies that had dissolved into tense and peevish errands, the train set in the cellar and before that the unfilled book of stamps and before that the model *Spirit of St. Louis* that was supposed to use real gas but never left the drafting table in the garage where they'd begun to put it together. The man led them to a corner the boy hadn't fully explored and stopped at a large tank with a single school in it, a cloud of identical fish, each one small as a razor blade and glinting with blue and red stripes, smaller than the boy had expected but beautiful in their brightness, in the way their name fit perfectly as his own, the school drifting slow as a vapor and then darting into fast motion when it turned, a haze of pink reflecting in the chubby man's face—*They like company, so you're gonna want at least seven*—and then his father in a businesslike voice asking the boy which one he liked best. Shyly, to please his father, he pointed at one that seemed a tiny bit bigger than the rest, its tail a vivid, deeper red, like the streak of a marker, and the chubby man lifted the lid of the tank and dunked a plastic bag so that it filled with water and began scooping the fish with his net, reaching down into the school and snaring two or three at once and then gloving his hand into the net to wiggle them into the bag. The man repeated the process until there were seven fish in all, lifting the bag of pinkly glowing water and offering it to the boy, a bulb of beautiful fish, but his father—stern and frowning, the space between his brows clamped to a quotation mark—gestured at the tank and made the man try again, pointing at the fish with the reddest tail, showing the man where to scoop the net, guiding him like a coach, once and then twice and then three times but it was always the wrong fish, until the moles on the man's face gleamed with sweat and he snapped, *For Christ sake, mister, they all look the same, what do you want?* to which his father went stiff and grabbed the net from the man's hands and tried to snare the fish himself, stabbing at the school until he'd dipped his sleeve into the water, his face burning with anger and impatience but also something else, a girlish blush that had been growing since he'd entered the store and was hard to distinguish from his sunburn (the boy, helplessly, wanting to button his father's shirt back up), the school of fish scattering each time his father swiped the net, as he came up again and again with the wrong catch, the one he sought forever darting from his reach, the cloud of fish opening and then closing, opening and closing, like a heart, a restless, solitary organ beating behind the glass: neon tetra, neon tetra.

Legends

DESMOND STOOD ON THE BAL-cony and looked down at the city: a lovely place smelling of piss, wedged into a ravine like the ruins of a landslide. Sun shone off the muddled roofs. The houses climbing the ravine were old and crooked, appealing in their anarchy, crammed together like an Englishman's teeth. A maze of a city, straight from a fairy tale. All considered, Desmond ranked it about a 7 on the untimely-death scale. That was how he tended to judge cities—whether he wouldn't mind dying there unexpectedly. What if he dropped dead in some godforsaken place he couldn't stand? At home, too, he had the same fear, worried he might keel over in a drugstore or Blockbuster video.

Early morning, but the Plaza de la Paz was already filling with people, churchgoers dressed up awkwardly and crowding the steps of the cathedral. The plaza of peace. They'd been in Mexico four days now and he hadn't seen anything very peaceful, just crowded streets and TVs blaring in the afternoon and alleys so tight they made him think of coronary thrombosis. The brochure had said: *Treat your ears to the melodious chime of church bells.* He was treating them now, but all he heard was the sound of explosives, men blasting the earth to a clamor of barking dogs.

"It's eight a.m.," Meredith called from inside the room. "What are they doing?"

"I don't know. Blasting the mines, probably."

"On a Sunday?" She groaned into her pillow. "I thought this was a Catholic country."

The blasts stopped and a cloud of swallows swooped under the balcony and rose in the air before dipping again, the tall flock folding over like a page. The birds flew down and darkened a tree. Desmond walked back into the hotel room. It was a nice room, bright-walled and colonial and not too elegant, large enough that the curtains flew out in a breeze. It was the balcony—the crumbling glamour of it—that had won Meredith's heart. "I feel like somebody's mistress," she'd said their first night in town, drinking sangria on the balcony while an *estudiantina* sang by in the street. She'd flashed him a tipsy look, though Desmond couldn't help wondering whose mistress she imagined being.

Naked, Meredith got out of bed and leaned over the dresser for her watch—a slim and graceful sight, though no more miraculous than the swallows. She'd stopped being a miracle last year, around the time Desmond caught her shaving her toes with his electric razor.

"What are they mining?" Meredith asked.

"Precious metals, I think. Used to be a silver town."

"Now it's a café town, I guess."

"They all are," Desmond said.

She yawned, squinting out the window. "Sunny again, do you believe it? Meteorology must be a dying art down here."

Desmond padded to the bathroom and took a Mexican piss, or so he'd come to consider it: long and desultory, the stream of Corona leaving him as leisurely as it had entered. The last time Meredith and Desmond had gone on a trip—four years ago—they'd stayed at a resort in the Caribbean and discovered a dead body in the swimming pool. This was during their honeymoon. They'd been drinking at the pool bar with the other guests, standing waist-deep in the water with their drinks, when Desmond had waded across the shallow end and felt something strange underfoot. A large shape, blunt and cumbersome. Without thinking, he'd reached into the cloudy water and pulled a man's leg from the bottom like a fish. He'd tugged on the leg, more startled than anything, but it was rooted in place and wouldn't budge. Meredith swam over and yelled for help and they kept pulling on the leg long after it was hopeless, refusing to believe anyone could drown in three feet of water. Eventually, some men in white polo shirts had to wheel out a pump and empty the pool. Meredith went back to their room, blue-lipped and shivering, but Desmond waited to see who it was: a pool cleaner from the hotel, snared to his elbow in the grate of a drain.

"Couldn't he have kicked his legs?" asked Meredith that night, too upset to sleep. But obviously, he *had* kicked. He'd kicked and kicked and kicked, but the people above him hadn't noticed.

Now here they were in Mexico, trying to have the honeymoon they'd deserved. Meredith had put on a bathrobe and was sitting bare-legged on the balcony.

"El Museo de las Momias," she said, cradling the guidebook between her knees. "The mummy museum. I want to go there before the day gets too hot."

"Since when were you interested in mummies?"

"It says it's famous." She looked up from the book. "I'm sure there are less touristy things. It's just a matter of finding them."

"We can't even find our hotel," Desmond said. Yesterday, in search of a restaurant, they'd gotten so lost in the warren of alleys that they'd spent half the afternoon roaming in circles, their stomachs growling like wolves. "Anyway, you need a guide for that stuff, someone who speaks Spanish. No one understands a word I'm saying. They just keep bringing me new forks."

Meredith leaned back in her chair. "I thought you'd be excited about the mummies. You're so hung up on death and dying and all that."

"Me?"

"Come on. Who else reads the obituaries *online*?"

Desmond tried to smile, watching the crowd of worshippers funnel into church. Lately, some funny things had been happening in his chest. He'd be stretching at home after a run or meeting with some clients at work when his heart would skip a beat, then frog-leap gently against his rib cage. It was subtle and alarming. He'd gone to see a cardiologist, a bored-looking man who'd shown him a remarkable film of his heart, a close-up of his valves and ventricles. It was like an avant-garde version of *The Blob*. During the screening, the cardiologist had told Desmond not to worry, that his valves were tight as a drum.

"Mild arrhythmia," he'd said, glancing at his watch. "As of yet, no cause for alarm."

"As of yet?"

"Your heart's a little lazier than some people's. Gets tired and loses its rhythm once in a while."

But Desmond couldn't help being alarmed. He could deal with a lazy eye, or even a lazy lung. But the heart was supposed to be a drastic workaholic. He was only thirty-one, though he'd heard about people dying from slacker hearts, collapsing one day while bending to tie a shoe.

"Anyway, try not to be so doom-and-gloom this trip," Meredith said now, standing to kiss him. He hadn't told her about his heart: one secret he'd managed to keep hidden. "This is our back-to-romance time. I don't want to blow it by being all sullen. I want to have adventures we can talk about when we're old together."

"I thought we were trying to *avoid* those," Desmond said. She pulled away from him and leaned over the city, frowning. "I just mean, hey, this is our second chance."

In San Francisco, Desmond worked for an ad agency called Product: Reality. His job was to come up with founding myths for various household products. *They told him it couldn't be done, but retracing the path of his ancestors to the bodegas of Modena, Italy, Stan Lugliani had a dream for a better domestic vinegar—rich, well-matured, savoring of integrity, like the old world itself.* Desmond didn't mind seeing his words on the backs of vinegar bottles. Sometimes he even convinced himself it was a good and worthy thing, turning ordinary men into heroes. For all he knew, Stan Lugliani might have had a dream of vinegar, though he had a sneaking suspicion it was just a name someone had cooked up in the marketing department. Italian, of course—but with a homey midwestern forename.

Everything had a legend these days. Desmond's latest assignment was the Zylar stud sensor, a home-improvement tool that looked like a ray gun from one of those old UFO movies. You could point it at a wall, and it would beep at the first detection of a stud. He'd been racking his brain for a week, trying to think of a legend, but couldn't find the right blend of utility and pathos. *After damaging the walls of his daughter's room, trying to hang a hook for her crutches, Bob Zylar decided to create a better tool—one that he could count on for his family.*

Desmond did his job as a copywriter and tried not to dwell on it. Still, when anyone asked about his work, he felt a vague creeping sickness and sometimes left out the "copy" part. At parties, especially, he was apt to stretch the truth.

"Oh? Do I know anything you've written?"

"The legend of Zylar."

The person—a web designer usually, because they all were—would mutter the name to himself with his head bowed in thought. "*Zylar*? Is that part of the Lair of the Serpent trilogy?"

Now, strolling down to the *jardín* with his wife, Desmond imagined the legend he'd write to describe their own humble beginnings. *After meeting the girl of his dreams, the loveliest midwife in town, Desmond failed to preserve her from his own mild failure and discovered his heart had aged improbably.* The sun leaned into his face. They had to walk in the middle of the street because the sidewalks were too crowded with churchgoers, drowsy-looking families hugging the margin of shade. (In the afternoons, when the shade crossed the street, everyone swarmed to one side and the town looked deserted from certain windows.) Desmond stared at the colonial roofs and strenuous, Escher-like stairways, wondering how the heart attack rate compared to America's. The only stores open on Sunday morning were the *taquerías,* men tending the spits already in their aprons, wielding knives long as swords and sculpting their gleaming diamonds of pork. Meredith studied the guidebook as they walked and kept a full stride ahead of Desmond, the camera swinging at her hip. She was wearing a straw hat she'd bought at a gift shop and loose-fitting pants to protect her legs. She had "Nordic Viking skin," like her mother. In the Caribbean, Meredith had sunburned her feet so badly she'd had to sleep with her ankles submerged in a wine bucket of water. Lying there naked in the morning, she'd seemed like an exotic dying plant. Now she looked more like a tulip, pretty but commonplace, her hat dwarfing the stalk of her with its droopy, king-size petals.

They ate breakfast at a café in the *jardín,* mopping their

food with tortillas while mariachis sang out requests. Desmond had never heard music so despairing in his life; the musicians were old and played as if their lives depended on it, which perhaps they did. When they found a request, the lead singer stood right at the table and shook his head while he sang, sewing tales of loss and disconsolate drinking, clutching his chest when he got to the chorus. In American restaurants you listened to Vivaldi, talked about the price of housing. Here, death sat down with you over eggs and wrung its beauty in your ear.

Mi vida no vale naadaaaa . . .

Meredith clapped politely after each song, joining the applause of the other tourists. She started talking to someone at the next table, a tan-faced American wearing huaraches and an indigenous wedding shirt embroidered with leafy shapes. Desmond knew it was a wedding shirt because he'd met other tourists in similar souvenirs, dressed like Oaxacan grooms, all of whom had paid "market prices" in remote Mexican villages. None of them seemed to be married.

"The mummies are a real trip. You know, they have the smallest mummy in the world, a little newborn like a Chihuahua." The fellow laughed. He was young but had the drowsy, world-weary squint of a seasoned traveler. "And a pregnant mummy, which I don't know but if you ever had an aching desire to see one."

"Are you just passing through?" Meredith asked.

"No, I wouldn't say that. Not by ordinary standards." He jerked a thumb at the alley behind them. "I teach English right down there, if you're familiar with it. At the Anglo Institute."

"Sounds like a neo-Nazi think tank," Desmond muttered.

"*¿Mande, amigo?*" The man cupped his fingers to his ear.

"The Anglo Institute. Anglo Youth?"

The man looked at him blankly. "There used to be a German guy working there, Buddendorf his name was, but he had *turista* so bad they booted him from the joint he was living in. Two weeks of nature calling and it was disturbing the other guests."

"Is that common?" Meredith asked, concerned.

"Take your chances, right?" He glanced at their empty plates. "Once I got the amoeba so bad in Chiapas I dragged my sleeping bag into the bathroom of a posada and crashed there for four days."

Desmond wondered if he was supposed to be impressed. Their first day here they'd met an Australian woman at the bakery; she'd told them triumphantly about spending three hours on a bus to Antigua, praying for a car wreck and clenching her sphincter.

"Maybe you can tell us how to get to the museum," Meredith said, changing the subject. She was great with strangers, travel agents, Jehovah's Witnesses—a trait Desmond both admired and resented. "We rented a car, but the book only tells you how to get there by bus."

"¿Qué tipo? One of those Bugs?"

"Jetta. The rental guy said we'd live longer."

The man picked a crumb from the tablecloth. "Of course, buses are the way to go ordinarily. I mean, if you're wanting to see the real Mexico."

"They're not dangerous?"

He laughed. "Not around here, at least. No bandidos. Unless you mind sharing your seat with a chicken."

The man stood up and introduced himself, pronouncing the name William with three syllables, like "trillium." He had a moon-shaped scar at the corner of his eye that waned to a sliver when he grinned. The locals called him Memo—short for Guillermo. He was just thinking, hey if they'd like, he could probably drive with them up to the museum. Mexicans weren't too good with signs and the roads were a little, what? . . . unmanicured sometimes. He chuckled in his throat, a bleak and rusty sound, like the deliberation of a frozen sink. At least he understood his own jokes. "I wouldn't crowd you guys, normally, but my niece is in town for a week and it's her last day to see the museum."

"Why not?" Meredith said uneasily, glancing at Desmond. He gave her a kick under the table, but she chose to ignore it. "William doesn't seem like a too bad criminal name."

"Call me Memo, please." The man spoke to her without looking at Desmond. "It's better to take the bus, like I said, but on a Sunday morning you never know—could end up waiting in the sun all day like a burro. Depends when the drivers fall out of bed, *entiendes*?"

"Memo isn't even a name," said Desmond, after dropping their valuables off at the hotel. "I think he got it from one of those prison movies on TV . . . like Mancini. There's always some rapist named Mancini or Sick Eddie."

"He seems like a perfectly nice guy." Meredith shrugged, smearing sunblock into her arm. "He's a little weird, I'll admit it. But he knows his way around. You said yourself you wish we had a guide."

"I'm not doubting his navigational skills."

"So what do you have against him?"

"It's that shirt. And the way he drops in those little Spanish phrases." Plus he could roll his *R*s—Desmond had been trying to do that since high school.

"What's he going to do?" she joked. "Pin me in the backseat while his niece defiles you at gunpoint? Where's your sense of adventure?"

It was something Desmond had fallen in love with, originally: Meredith's acceptance of people, her willingness to give anyone a chance. Her "good shepherdess streak," Desmond called it. It was chummy and munificent but also got in the way of things, like a Great Dane at a party. Once, when they'd first started dating, Meredith made them pick up a hitchhiker outside the Safeway, a boy with extravagant piercings all over his face. He looked as if he'd been dragged across the bottom of a fishing hole. The boy spent the whole ride talking about his girlfriend's various allergies and then ended up stealing some groceries from the backseat. "There's sesame in the granola," Meredith had said afterward, worried about his girlfriend. Her dream in life was to start a nonprofit birthing center for teenage mothers. Desmond had told Meredith his dreams too, how he'd wanted to be a writer in college and had written a twenty-two-page love poem.

"A love poem?" she'd said, interested. "What about?"

"Orpheus and Eurydice—except like an updated thing. A contemporization?" He was embarrassed for having mentioned it. "He's a jazz trumpeter and she's a travel agent."

"Do they whatever? She die tragically and he try to woo her back from Hades with his trumpet?"

"No. It's abstract."

"Abstract?"

"A metaphor. They're doomed in the same way."

"I've always wondered about that," she'd said thoughtfully. "All these stories about doomed lovers who can't be together. Star-crossed, right?" She touched his leg and smiled. "What about the rest of them, the star-pleased ones, who wake up every day and use each other's toothbrush?"

Those days, before Desmond and Meredith were married, they'd made love every chance they got. In the kitchen, off the trail of a hike, in the back of his car like resourceful teenagers. They'd broken things and torn clothes without thinking. Pagan deeds, brave and rambunctious. If someone had told them they'd lose interest, the way it seemed now, they would have laughed out loud. In fairness, part of it was their schedule. Meredith was on delivery call at the hospital, which meant she disappeared several nights a week and rarely got home before dawn. Desmond would be just waking up for work, stumbling out of bed when she crawled under the covers and stole his pillow. All that time crouched at other people's beds made her proprietorial of her own.

"Tomorrow," they'd promise each other groggily, knocking heads sometimes in their sleepiness.

But often when a day off came they neglected their promise, preferring the cozy evasion of domestic chores. At night they spooned together in bed and lay there without moving, Meredith falling asleep in the clasp of his arms, like a textbook illustration of the Heimlich maneuver. Perhaps, Desmond feared, there was a shelf life to desire. Sooner or later, the erotic mystery dried up and you wanted to sleep with someone who didn't use your toothbrush.

Now Meredith was humoring some weirdo with an embroidered shirt, in the same way she'd indulged the hitchhiker from the grocery store. Desmond was hoping he wouldn't show up, but there he was in the *jardín*, wearing the same outfit and snaking through the crowd to greet them. He shook Desmond's hand politely and kissed Meredith hello on the cheek. She blushed a bit, explaining how they'd decided to leave the car at the hotel for adventure's sake. For someone who preferred the bus, he looked strangely disappointed. (Of course, his niece had decided to leave town early and wouldn't be joining them.) The three of them boarded the rickety bus when it came and took the only seats left, some damaged ones near the back, which shook and chattered on the rock-strewn road until Desmond felt old Spanish words dislodge from his brain and flutter around like bats. *Mensaje . . . cinturón . . . orgulloso.* Flash cards from his youth. Other passengers craned their necks to look at him and Meredith, their sunburned faces etched in thought. One of them—a grave and dignified old man—had on a baseball cap that said: IF ASSHOLES COULD FLY, THIS PLACE WOULD BE AN AIRPORT.

At the museum, Memo insisted on paying for their tickets, waving his hand when Desmond took out his wallet and performing the transaction in Spanish. The three of them split up to look at the mummies. The rooms were dark and crowded, filled with bench-high pews that looked like places to sit before Desmond realized they were the main attraction. Not pews at all but display cases, row after row of them, coffins topped with glass so you could view the corpses, people dried stiff as leather or withered to question marks. Desmond toured the rows by himself and inspected the mummies. Like any evidence of death, they were exotic or thrilling in the abstract, but once you saw things with your own eyes the repetitive drab logic of it made you queasy. There was a miner wearing boots, a pregnant woman with a deflated stomach, a dapper-looking man with a full beard and well-preserved penis. Some of the people were less intact than others, meaning you could see into the hollows of their bodies, the skin smashed or peeling like the ruins of a piñata. One exhibit in particular caught Desmond's attention. A group of tourists near the farthest wall, crowded around a trophy case balanced on a plinth. Desmond waited in line to get a look, intrigued and appalled at the same time, guessing it was the world's smallest mummy that Memo had boasted of. Inside the case, sure enough, was a premature baby smaller than a kitten. The baby's eyes were shut, its hands still curled from the womb. The baby's skin was all black and shriveled; underneath, poking through almost, you could see the meticulous matchwork of its ribs. It was like looking at an angel grilled on a skewer. The baby's arms were reaching above its head, gnarled into branches, as though trying to climb back into the womb.

Desmond felt dizzy, hollowed out himself. He moved off and watched the other tourists examine the mummy, their faces bending over the trophy case. One of them—a man in skimpy shorts and knee-high socks—took his glasses off to inspect the mummy and then hooted in surprise. He turned and said something to his companion, who burst out laughing. Desmond saw the same sort of behavior throughout the museum, people pointing at the cases and joking with their neighbors. Were they that content with their future? Following the arrows to the next room, he glanced back and saw a foreign woman leaning over an exhibit behind him. He couldn't see her face, but she was tall and beautifully gawky, a gangling blonde dressed in white. The nape of her neck was damp with sweat, a strand of hair curled there like a sea horse. When she looked up, Desmond saw that it was Meredith. She was chatting with Memo. It was the strangeness of it, the surprise of seeing her with another man that had caused him to mistake her. She looked beautiful even now, clutching her hat in one hand, and the sweat in her hair filled him with longing.

Desmond got outside and sat on the curb. He felt his heart pull in his chest, once, like a current. At least he thought he felt it—who knew for sure? He sat there for a time before looking up from the road and seeing Memo and Meredith leave the museum together, dazed but smiling, their eyes squinting in the sunlight.

"There's Mexico for you," Memo said, holding Meredith's arm. "No pussyfooting around death like we do back home."

"Pussyfooting?" she asked.

"What we do in America. It's like spiritual fascism—repress everything until it becomes a neurosis. Here it's out in the open, *abierto,* where it can breathe." He grinned and turned to Desmond. "*¿Qué te pasa?* Did they bore you, *amigo?*"

· · ·

That night Memo took them to a cantina he liked, a nameless place tucked down an alley not mentioned in their guidebook. Desmond had always thought the term "hole-in-the-wall" was a metaphor. But here was a hole knocked literally out of a wall, arched like a cave and crumbling from the wreckage. A giant mouse den throbbing with music. Memo ushered them to a plastic table by the corner and ordered three of the same thing before Desmond could stop him. The bartender seemed to recognize Memo, clapping him on the back and crooning something in the melodic singsong of street vendors.

"I thought women weren't allowed in these places," said Meredith, clearly enthralled.

"Only Mexican women. It's a domestic thing, *la mala mujer*." Memo leaned over the table and gestured at the other patrons, aging businessmen with slicked-back hair, drinking Coronas and chatting with their sleeves rolled up. "I've taken foreign women here before, so don't worry about the *machos*."

Desmond wondered how many of Memo's women had been married. The bartender poured three shots from a bottle, and Memo got up and collected them without paying a cent. Did he wink at the bartender—or was it just Desmond's imagination? Less than a day had passed and he already hated this walking Spanish phrase book. "It's our last chance to get off the Gringo Trail," Meredith had said earlier, chiding Desmond for not wanting to come along. True enough, he thought—though he was beginning to suspect the Gringo Trail was a condition more than a travel route, something you kicked in front of you despite yourself, like Buster Keaton chasing his hat.

Memo sat down with the drinks, and for the first time Desmond noticed the roots of his hair: they were pale brown, lighter than the jet black of his bangs. "I was thinking tomorrow I might take you to see *la Niña Milagrosa*."

"What's that?" Meredith asked.

"The miracle girl. Name's Elba, supposedly, but nobody calls her that." Memo explained how the girl lived on a ranch nearby and had been bedridden for fourteen years—not comatose but dead to the world, inert and helpless, the result of a riding accident from when she was small. She couldn't talk or respond to people at all. She was said to perform miracles and attracted pilgrims from all over the country. "That's how she communicates—by performing these miracles. The parents say she gets stigmata on her hands during holy days."

"Probably one of those awkward teen things," Desmond said.

"A 'victim soul,' they call her, which means she suffers for people and asks God to heal them."

"We've already made plans tomorrow, unfortunately."

Memo downed his shot and leaned toward Meredith. "Get this? The whole house? It's filled with these homemade gifts and souvenirs, crutches from people who've been cured on the spot."

"We're going to San Miguel tomorrow," Desmond said, "spending the night."

"*Bueno.* The ranch is right on the way out of town. They only take visitors in the morning, so we'll show a leg early."

Either he wasn't listening or all that polluted Mexican water had gone to his brain. Desmond felt like a stiff for resisting, but he couldn't help himself. "Look, miracle girls aren't our thing. We don't believe in that crap."

"Des, for Christ sake," Meredith said, blushing.

"What?"

"What do you have against miracles all of a sudden?"

"Everything." To believe in them, for one, you had to admit illness was a vicious prank.

"Well, *I'm* interested in seeing this *milagrosa* girl—it's not like we have to be anywhere do or die." She turned to Memo.

"Des hasn't felt well since the museum," she said. "The mango for breakfast, we think."

Desmond drank the shot of tequila in front of him, bowing to a sudden need to prove himself. It tasted like the brine left in a pickle jar. He'd barely set the glass down before his body churned in protest, a seismic groan rising from his bowels— much like the desire he'd felt twisting in his stomach all afternoon. Honestly, he was having a hard time telling the difference. Meredith was wearing a gauzy chiffon skirt, sheer enough to convey the whiteness of her legs.

"You don't seem like you're married," Memo said, peering at them gravely. "The resemblance." He frowned into his glass. "I've noticed the married tourists down here, how their faces always look like one another."

Desmond laughed. "You're saying marriage causes deformity?"

"That's what the old Nahua people believed. This gringo hippie gave me a book about them. The Nahuas from right here where we're cozy-time chatting. They had this idea that we're born with the wrong face, like an impostor's, that the heart has to combine some way with the face and get rid of it." He leaned forward to give his words drama. "It's the whole reason for being on earth: to try and make a face that goes with your heart."

"What happens if you can't make the right face?" Meredith asked.

"Most people can't. They just wander around trying on faces."

Desmond had to admit it was a good myth, much more compelling than his tales of American success. All he ever wrote about were people getting rich. He wanted to write something with truer odds, a legend about failure.

"And you?" Meredith asked. "Were you ever married?"

Memo laughed. "No chance, *señora*. I like controlling my own face."

He signaled to the bartender, who came over with three more shots. It occurred to Desmond that he'd dyed his hair in order to look more Mexican. Memo and Meredith lifted their glasses to compare portions, draining the tequila like cowboys. Desmond gave his shot to Memo, who drank half of it and passed the rest to Meredith across the table.

"Besides, it's against human nature," Memo said. "Monogamy. There's a proverb in Mexico: 'Don't let your hens run loose in the yard when the rooster's out.' " He leaned toward Meredith again, a confidential crouch, his thumb stabbing the air in Desmond's direction. "*Dígame,* honestly. Haven't you ever worried about your rooster here?"

Meredith sniffed her tequila and reflected for a minute, her eyebrows peaked. "No. I don't think I have."

To his surprise, Desmond sensed that she wasn't altogether happy about this. A man ducked through the entrance of the bar, nervously, and Memo watched him for a second as he made his way past the tables and slid into a corner. The man looked out of place among the businessmen, a campesino carrying something back from the market, wearing huaraches and an old Members Only windbreaker. Desmond inspected the dead thing in his hand, saw it was actually a machete. The campesino caught Desmond's eye and then looked at the floor.

"A student of mine. *Disculpe.*"

Memo got up casually and went over to the corner, greeting the man without smiling. They shook hands in a professional manner. While they were talking, the bartender came over to the table again and cleared Desmond's and Meredith's empty glasses.

"*Aguas, señores,*" the bartender said in his musical accent, leaning toward them. He added something that Desmond didn't understand, dragging his *E*s out indulgently, like a cat stretching. Desmond thought he shot a glance at the empty chair.

"What did he say?" Meredith asked.

"Aguas." Desmond looked at Memo in the corner, who waved at them and formed a *momentito* signal with his fingers. "Be careful."

"He means the tequila," she said, closing her eyes. She opened them after a minute and peered at Desmond with her forehead rumpled. He wondered, sadly, if this were the face she was meant to grow into. "He's got the wrong person. You don't need any help in the careful department."

Later, drunk, she danced with Memo, swaying to the salsa rhythms on the jukebox. She turned her ankle on a stray bottle and held his shoulder for balance. Desmond was too sick to stand, wanting to go home but also transfixed by the wobble of her grin, how one side of her mouth curled higher than the other. Had he never noticed it before? The erotic slant of her smile? Perhaps he was feverish, but it seemed to him mysterious and startling, an improbable discovery, like finding a bird's egg in a coat you haven't worn for years. Some men at the bar catcalled at the dancers, and Desmond pressed his hand to his shirt, his heart stumbling once like their steps.

On the way home, Meredith walked a few steps ahead and veered drunkenly up the *callejón* to their hotel. The sound of her heels echoed off the walls, clacking in different places than her footsteps. Crouched and feeble-headed, Desmond had the brief but sorrowful impression he was trailing a ghost. There was so much, suddenly, he wanted to say. He wanted to say that he loved her, that the rest of his life was bill paying and stud sensors and a moon-blind distraction from death, that he hadn't achieved anything worthwhile except marrying a woman who picked up hitchhikers from the grocery store. "You hurt yourself salsaing," he found himself saying instead, watching her limp up the stairs to their hotel room.

"Funny, isn't it? I didn't even notice."

In their room, Desmond hunched to the bathroom and washed his face, making sure to seal his lips as he splashed. Later, glancing in the mirror, he noticed something peculiar about his mouth. A darkness where his teeth should be, like the mummies' vacant screams. He stuck out his tongue. It was black and hideous, coated in a chalky film that had spread to his gums. What was happening to him? He scratched his tongue with a fingernail, vigorously, but it didn't leave a mark.

"It's a sign maybe," Meredith said, unalarmed. The tequila had made her blasé.

"What do you mean?"

"You miss American cuisine. Burritos."

"Meredith, Jesus. This is serious. I don't believe in signs."

"That's right. No signs. No miracles." She flumped back on the bed. "What do you believe in?" She asked this honestly, without glibness.

"Lots of things. A healthy tongue."

"Besides that."

"Lots of things."

"Name one, could you?"

He stared at the bedpost. For some reason he thought of the baby at the museum, the mummified newborn with its arms stretched eternally behind it. "Wombsickness," he said finally.

Meredith looked at him strangely, the slant of her smile frayed into a squiggle. Desmond lay down beside her. She took his hand unexpectedly and held it near her hip. The ceiling fan was revolving at low speed, making a doggish whine as it turned. He laid his hand on her shoulder, and she turned toward him with her eyes closed. Her face surprised him: dampcheeked and snowy, sprinkled with tiny feathers from her pillow. She pressed against him, softly at first and then more firmly, the smell of other men's cigarettes in her hair, and they moved together for a minute before Desmond had to stop, tuned to the slightest quirk or tremor in his chest, the whirl of nausea expanding in his head.

"It's not you," he said. "There's something wrong with my heart."

She let go of him and closed her eyes, nodding faintly through her feathers, as if he were confirming something she already knew.

The ranch was high in the mountains outside of town. Desmond sat in the backseat behind Memo, who'd insisted on driving because of "loose cattle"—Desmond had imagined long-lashed heifers leaning against a fence and mooing seductively from the side of the road. The road was weedy and unpaved, and the Jetta lost purchase occasionally in the dirt, weighed down by their luggage in the trunk. The guidebook had cautioned against leaving anything at the hotel—one of the "Ten Commandments of Theft Prevention"—but now Desmond wondered if they shouldn't have left everything behind. He was still queasy but felt much better than yesterday, fasting after the night's turmoil in his stomach, which had subsided to a low but constant simmer. Meredith relaxed in the front seat with her head slumped against the headrest, nursing a hangover and a swollen ankle. She'd refused to let them miss the trip. "I guess honeymoons aren't our forte," she'd said matter-of-factly, limping as Desmond helped her to the car.

They drove through land sparse as a Dalí painting and climbed eventually to a settlement with homemade basketball nets and wood shanties pushing up smoke and more commodious dwellings shaded with palm trees. It was a breezy day, and the palm trees sculled their fronds in the wind. Desmond kept his window rolled up and tried not to stare at people crowding their porches. He felt nostalgic for minimalls. He glanced in the rearview mirror and examined his tongue, which hadn't changed since last night.

"Have you been eating Pepto-Bismol?" Memo asked, catching his eye from the front seat. Desmond blushed and stuck in his tongue. "That's the trouble with those things. The tablets. Turn your whole tongue black."

The miracle girl lived in an abandoned cowshed at the end of the road. As they neared the shed, a trio of dogs converged from different ends of the yard and chased the car to a halt, circling like wolves, jumping at the windows and gnashing their teeth. The dogs were small but ferocious. Memo pulled a firecracker from his pocket, lit the fuse with the car lighter, and then threw the firecracker out the window, alarming the dogs, which scattered in several directions at the blast. Rabies prevention, he called it. Beside the cowshed, close to the road, was a large hole dug into the ground and mounded on one side with dirt, an unhinged door lying in the scrub beside it. A ladder peeked out of the hole, forming an H against the dirt.

"What are they digging?" Desmond asked, wondering in grim amazement if it were a grave.

"A well, probably," Memo said. "*Agua's* got legs—a moving target out here."

The three of them got out of the car, and a woman in a sleeveless tunic appeared from behind the shed. The woman looked cross, holding a sopping dress in front of her. Memo told Desmond and Meredith to wait by the car and approached the woman privately. Outside the tourist realm of the city, Memo looked quaint and Californian, the back pocket of his Levi's ripped and dog-eared to a darker blue. The woman looked away when he spoke, wringing the dress with two hands and spitting in the dirt. Her face was stern and motionless.

"I had to tell her you were sick. Only chronic cases are allowed to see her right now." Memo shrugged at Desmond and smiled at the ground. He seemed dejected, as though it was his own fault the woman hadn't rushed over to greet them. Of course, Meredith was right: he wasn't dangerous at all, just some American with dyed hair wanting to please them. "You go first," Memo said, trying to be enthusiastic. "We'll wait outside and talk her into letting Meredith have a look when you're done."

Desmond glanced at Meredith, who seemed put off by the woman's unfriendliness. What the hell were they doing here? It was pushy and somehow feudal, this brand of tourism. Desmond wanted to throw Meredith in the car and skid away with his hand on her leg, a Clyde Barrow rescue, driving all night until they saw the splendid billboards of Texas rising above them. Certainly he didn't want to barge into this family's house and watch some poor girl drool on her pillow. Still, it would seem silly—*careful*—to refuse.

He grinned at them, to show how adventurous he was, before striding off to the house.

Ducking under the lintel of the doorway, he entered the main part of the shed, a huge, spartan room with several beds pushed against the wall like a dormitory. A man was sitting at a table by the window, eating something from a plastic bowl. He glanced up between bites and nodded at Desmond. The man's eyes were pink and rheumy-looking, familiar as a déjà vu, though Desmond couldn't say how they'd met. Hanging on the wall behind him were crude paintings of Virgin Marys and nativity scenes and crucified Jesuses in varying stages of distress, their faces white as Norwegians'. Streaks of reddish goo flowed from the Virgins' eyes or else seeped from the middles of the paintings. The goo looked like drips of ketchup. Beneath the paintings, propped against the wall, was a collection of medical devices, crutches and discarded braces and even a child's wheelchair transformed into an altar, woven with flowers and covered with candles picturing saints. Desmond wondered how a child, resurrected from a lifetime of paralysis, would be able to sprint past the dogs outside.

"*Por allá,*" the man said, pointing at an oak door wedged between the beds.

Besides the entrance, it was the only door in the room. Desmond walked to the door and opened it and ducked down a hallway that looked like it went to an old dairy room, half thinking it would lead to some back-world dungeon, a room of enslaved visitors and starving cripples begging for their crutches.

He reached the end of the hall and stopped in his tracks.

He wasn't prepared for what he saw. He wasn't prepared for the stillness of the girl, lying in a bed with two railings boxing her in like a crib. She lay there in the sunlight, wrapped in a blanket and staring at the wall done over with *retablos,* tin cards painted with her image and thanking her for cures. There was a bag, filled with what looked like café au lait, dangling from a pole beside her. A tube vined down the pole and disappeared into her stomach. The girl was bad-skinned and homely but had long, glamorous black hair, the most beautiful hair Desmond had ever seen, hanging off the edge of the bed in finely brushed locks. A little boy was kneeling by the bed, trimming her hair with a pair of scissors and putting the cuttings in a box.

Desmond stepped into the room, which smelled mossy. The boy looked at him for a second and then resumed snipping the girl's hair, ducking his head again without flinching. The tin box where he put the cuttings had a cross stamped into low relief on the top.

"*Mi hermana habla con Dios,*" he said loudly, as if Desmond were hard of hearing. "Sister speak is God."

The boy's English impressed him, the gutsy imperfection of it. Desmond dared himself to approach the bed and crouched down beside the girl. Her face was sad-looking and blued with acne, slumped to one side on the pillow. Her eyes were still as a corpse's. Up close she seemed no more than a child, twelve or thirteen at the most—though her body looked older. Her mouth hung open on the pillow, as if waiting to be fed. A moth blundered at the makeshift window screen above them, the only sound in the room except for the scissors. It was the silence that was so disturbing. He understood how somebody might make up a story to explain it. You would create one from despair, from tedium even—and who in their right mind would ever blame you? He peered at the girl's eyes and thought he saw one of them flicker for a second, some thought's glimmer in her pupil, until Desmond realized it wasn't a thought at all but *him* he was seeing, a tiny, phantomlike face, his own reflection trapped in a globe of black.

He shrank back.

"My sister no rest," the boy said, pronouncing "sister" to rhyme with "beware." He'd stopped trimming the girl's hair and was standing under the *retablos* with the box of cuttings. "Is dream us in the sleep."

"She dreams us in her sleep," Desmond said, wondering if that was what he'd meant, the eerie absence of "about." He imagined the girl creating them in her sleep, actually dreaming their lives into existence, inventing the little room and mossy air and everything else in it. God, what labor! The breadth of detail was astounding. Take himself—his own body. Sure, she'd have to envision his face and teeth, his arms and legs and shoulders, but there were the less glamorous parts as well, the unsung bumps and corners: the knuckles of his toes, or that weird mole in his armpit, or even the invisible growth of his nails. She would have needed to start weeks . . . years ago, probably.

There would have been restless nights, products of whimsy or indigestion. How else to explain the bones in his ear? If she were truly dreaming him (and why not, since it made as much sense as anything?), then the hairs in his nose were a work of love, the result of extraordinary visions. And after all that dreaming, the toil and concentration, how could you blame her for getting tired one day and wanting to stop, for being too wiped out to continue?

It occurred to him that you could suggest something, whisper a message in the girl's ear, like those subliminal tapes you buy to stop smoking. You could influence her and change the dream.

And that was what he did now. He got on his knees and crouched beside the girl's face. He asked for his heart to get better, actually whispered it out loud to her ear. Then he asked for a new marriage with Meredith, imagining a house in the country for some reason, someplace like Vermont or New Hampshire where it snowed in the winter—a ranch like this maybe, but close enough to a town where they could still see movies. They'd spend winter Sundays in bed, blurry with lust. He'd find a job he could admit to strangers. It seemed to Desmond, kneeling on the hardpan dirt of the dairy room, that it would be possible—*easy*—to start their lives over, like actual newlyweds.

Moved by his whispering, the boy opened the tin box he was holding and gave Desmond a lock of hair, choosing it carefully and placing it in his hand like a pinch of tobacco. A souvenir. The girl's hair stuck to Desmond's fingers, which seemed to be trembling. He thanked the boy awkwardly and slid the hair into the pocket of his T-shirt.

There was a voice from the house. Desmond stood up, gripped by an unaccountable chill. The man at the table. He remembered, all at once, where he'd seen him before: Memo's "student," the campesino in the bar carrying the machete.

He edged toward the window screen, searching for his wife

in the yard. But Meredith wasn't there. She wasn't standing in the road, or anywhere else he could see. Desmond left the dairy room and rushed back down the hall and past the chair where the campesino had been sitting, scanning the empty room before finding the door. He ran blinded into the sun and searched for Meredith in the glare until her voice rose from the earth, calling his name in a muffled scream. A panicked voice, shrunk to an echo. He followed her cries and swung around the front of the cowshed until he faced the half-dug well, which was covered now with the door, the ladder yanked up and thrown to one side in the scrub. The dogs were leashed to a metal gate in the corral and, at the sight of Desmond, reared choking against their ropes. He opened his mouth to answer Meredith but something flashed in front of him and his voice stopped at his throat, snuffed by a sharp blow to his stomach, the jolt of pain sucking his words back like smoke. He dropped to all fours, gasping. A man's shadow shrank across the weeds and Memo bent down into the field of Desmond's vision, fixing the strap of a huarache that had slipped from his heel. His face was blurred by the sun. The pain crawled up Desmond's throat and he spat in the dirt, the slap of sandals running off behind him.

Wincing, Desmond stayed on all fours and struggled to breathe. He closed his eyes against the dust. His heart pounded in his chest, a faithful rhythm. Dazed, he focused on the thread of footsteps receding from his ears: how the keys in Memo's pocket jangled when he ran, like music, like the dwindling cadence of a song, stranding Desmond in the dirt and taking his belongings—his clothes, his passport, his ticket home— stealing everything he had except his wife, who called to him faintly, again and again, as if from another world.

A Fear of
Invisible Tribes

O N THE DAY OF HER SECOND DRIV-
ing lesson, Quinn waited in the car with
three other people while their instructor filled up the tank at
Gas 'N' Go. The gas station was small and deserted, a dumpy-
looking place with graffiti tagging the pumps. Through the window of the backseat, Quinn watched the instructor helplessly,
terrified at the prospect of braving the freeway for the first time.
The car was a stick shift, which only added to her terror. She
closed her eyes and tried to imagine herself at home, floating in
a warm bath while Bach's cello suites slithered from the kitchen.
("Guided imagery," her therapist called it.) Instead Quinn saw
herself with a blindfold on, cornered by pirates: a knock-kneed
captive, walking the plank and inching to her doom.

Quinn opened her eyes. She fidgeted in the backseat, sandwiched between a boy with green hair and a woman named Delaney. Delaney was Quinn's age, a recovering alcoholic who'd failed her driver's test three times in a row and finally gone back to school. Folded in her lap was a jean jacket with a picture of a golden retriever silk-screened on its back. Quinn examined it carefully, to steady her nerves. The golden retriever was looking off into the distance like Vermeer's lute player, bathed in a nimbus of softened light, the word REX scripted in rope lettering below it. In college, Quinn had once written a paper called "Visions of Home: Finding Ourselves in Rockwell's Caricature," but it seemed to her that even Norman Rockwell wouldn't have thought to capture Rex's *mal du pays*.

The boy in the driver's seat, a teenager with orange hair spiked to the roof, torqued his waist so he could lean into the backseat and address his friend. The two boys were in a perpetual state of disagreement. Quinn couldn't remember what their real names were, so she kept them apart by the color of their hair. Today they were arguing about the right way to make a hamburger.

"No way," Orange Boy was saying. "You put the tomato on first and *then* the lettuce. It keeps the bun from getting soggy."

"You don't know anything," Green Boy said. "That's totally fucked up."

"It's like a raincoat."

"It's not like a raincoat! It's like a lettuce!"

"Don't spit on me. Yuck, dude. You're spitting from your lips."

"Let's ask Ms. Professor," Green Boy said, turning to Quinn. His face was tan and earnestly pimpled. She regretted exaggerating now, telling them she was a teacher at Berkeley—how long had it been since she'd tried to impress a fifteen-year-old boy? "What do *you* think?"

"I don't eat hamburgers," Quinn mumbled.

"Me neither," Delaney said, nodding vigorously. She smiled

at Quinn: a toothy, eventful grin, as if she'd just popped out of a cake. "*E. coli.* It's like Russian roulette."

Green Boy stared at them. Quinn wondered if he believed she and Delaney were friends, ashamed at her eagerness to set him straight. Delaney liked to use terms like "drug of choice" and "black-and-white thinking." They'd met the first day of classroom training. Within minutes she'd told Quinn her whole life history, how she'd lived in six states before moving to San Francisco, where she'd been arrested for drunk driving and ended up in a residential treatment program. Now she was sober and trying to get her license back. Quinn took off her glasses, nervously, and began to clean them with her shirt. Without them, the Gas 'N' Go sign looked like an enormous fuzzball, suspended in midair.

"I'm not really a professor," she explained. Perhaps because these fearless-looking strangers would be putting their lives into her hands, she felt the need to clear up who she was. "I'm a grad student. Art history."

Delaney seemed to perk up. "Oh yeah? You didn't tell me they were art classes."

"Well, I'm done with classes. I'm writing my dissertation." Quinn glanced at her. "It's like a paper."

"What's it about?"

"Oh, nothing you'd care about." She'd meant it as a kind of compliment, but now she worried how she'd sounded. "This woman who did these organic shapes? Eva Hesse?"

"I'm an artist myself," Delaney said. "I mean, not a real one. I just doodle, really, but it helps keep me sane." She caught Quinn's eye and blushed. "I really like Jim Davis."

Quinn looked at her, surprised. She tried to place the name. Davis. It sounded all-American, like one of the Dia minimalists: Judd, Smithson. She felt ashamed for assuming a woman with a dog on her jacket knew nothing about art.

"You know him, right? *Garfield*? I could copy his stuff for hours."

The two boys, Orange and Green, smirked at each other. Quinn faced the window to avoid looking at them, watching the instructor screw the cap back on the gas tank and then amble sleepily over to the mini-mart to pay in cash. She couldn't wait to tell Keith about Jim Davis, feline primitivist. Keith was her brother, who'd bought her the driving lessons for her birthday. He'd given her his old stick-shift Volvo, knowing she couldn't drive—she'd never felt the need to learn in New York. But San Francisco was different: she'd lived here for four years and was always hounding Keith for rides. Quinn suspected he was sick of it, though sometimes she wondered if he'd enrolled her in driving school for his own entertainment. He loved hearing her reports on the phone, cackling at the instructor's bad breath or Delaney's talk-show babble.

The windows of the mini-mart reflected the sun so she couldn't see inside. What was taking so long? To calm herself, Quinn invoked a memory from college, part of a presentation she'd given for an anthropology class and which she recited to herself, like a psalm or a mantra, in times of dread. It was a description of the Nuer tribe of Africa. She loved the Nuer tribe—they had a range of fears broader than her own. They had, from what she remembered, over a thousand things to be scared about: a fear of spells, a fear of carnivores, a fear of misinterpretation, a fear of darkness, a fear of becoming trees, a fear of forgetting the names of the colors, a fear of invisible tribes, a fear of sums past ten.

The passenger door opened. Quinn smiled, trying to exude a semblance of composure, as their instructor climbed into the front seat. Except it wasn't the instructor. It was someone else.

The someone else was out of breath and holding a backpack and an umbrella. He lifted the umbrella, which turned out to be a shotgun sawed down to half its length.

"Okay," he said fiercely. "Get moving out of here!"

Orange Boy looked at him from the driver's seat, a withered pouch of bubble gum hanging from his lips.

"Drive!" the man said again, shaking the gun at his face.

Orange Boy started the car and then floored the gas, clutching the wheel and revving the car wildly in neutral. The man stared at him with his mouth open. Quinn thought about leaping from the car, but her heart was squirming so hard she couldn't move. Eventually, Orange Boy realized what was wrong, ground the shift terribly, and lurched into gear, sending the car on a whiplashing shudder toward the street and almost killing a pedestrian wheeling a bag of laundry down the sidewalk. He veered left and plowed through an abandoned shopping cart, then jumped over the curb, skidding onto Bayshore amid a glissando of honks before righting the wheels and hitting the gas. The engine roared like a tractor's. Orange Boy leaned forward and tried to shift into second, but the gearshift made a terrible zapping sound and he jerked his hand back, pulling over to the side of the road next to a parking meter.

"Jesus Christ," the man yelled, catching his breath, "can't you drive a car?"

Orange Boy let go of the wheel, visibly relieved. People screamed at them as they whooshed by in their cars. The man stared at him, blinking.

"Okay, you," he said, twisting toward the backseat and gesturing at Delaney. "Get up here behind the wheel!"

"I can't drive, either."

"What?"

"None of us can drive."

The man looked at her in disbelief. "What do you mean?"

"We're learning," she said. "This is a driver's-ed car." The man seemed not to hear her. *"Driving school,"* Delaney said carefully, pausing at each syllable.

The man looked at the twin rearview mirror centered in front of him. He dragged his free hand slowly down his face. For a minute, Quinn thought he might start crying.

"Of all the cars in the city, I steal one filled with people who can't drive?"

No one answered. The man turned toward the backseat again, studying the three of them more carefully before fixing on Green Boy, whose body had gone rigid next to Quinn's. The man's face seemed to sink even further.

"Why don't you let us out?" Green Boy said nervously. "You can let us out and drive yourself."

"I don't drive stick," he murmured. He glanced at the cars whipping by the window. "I don't believe this. What a fucking joke."

"It's an honest mistake," Green Boy said, gaining confidence. "Anyone could make it. How were you supposed to know?"

"Actually, there's a big sign on the back?" Orange Boy said from the driver's seat. "Like in yellow? *Caution: Student Driver?*"

"You could totally miss it, though," Green Boy said, flashing him a look.

"Yeah. Right. Like if you were in a big rush."

"Don't fuck with me!" the man yelled at them, jerking the sawed-off gun back and forth. Orange Boy's face turned white in the rearview mirror and dropped from view. The man licked his lips and glanced around desperately. "Who's the best driver in here?"

"Ms. Professor," Green Boy whispered.

Quinn shook her head. She tried to speak, but her throat had tightened like a fist.

"Okay, Professor! Get up here! Now! Don't try anything weird, or they'll be looking for a whatever tomorrow. Substitute."

Quinn needed to move, to follow the man's orders—but her body had frozen up and wouldn't heed her commands. Her heart was trapped in a helpless fury. The only thing she could control was her hand, which was gripping something warm at her side. She was squeezing it with all her strength. The man in the passenger seat peered out the window, anxiously, and then poked the shotgun inches from Quinn's face. A faint smell of cordite made her nose itch.

"It's your choice," he hissed. "Get up here behind the wheel or I'll kill you. Which do you want?"

Delaney leaned forward, staring him in the eyes. Her voice was slow and deliberate. "If you kill her, none of us will drive you anywhere. You'll have to kill all four of us."

The man's eyes darted around the car. He glanced at the roof, like someone realizing he was trapped in an elevator. The gun drooped in his hands. He stared at it longingly, as if it would tell him what to do. There was a lull in traffic, the car's engine ticking in the silence. To Quinn's astonishment, the man let the gun fall to his lap and slipped it under his T-shirt as best he could, like a stolen baguette. Then he fumbled out the door, peering up and down the street. He lunged across the street with his backpack, one arm tucked under his bulging shirt, a weirdly pregnant shape loping into an alley.

A wave of traffic covered his tracks. Orange Boy and Green Boy made sure he was gone before pulling out their cell phones and squabbling over who should call the police. Their faces were pink and excited. Quinn glanced down at the thing she was squeezing, realizing only then that it was Delaney's hand.

Their fingers were laced together, threaded like lovers'. Delaney unfroze first and tried to release her fingers, but Quinn didn't want to let go.

"She saved my life," Quinn told Keith on the phone.

"Sounds like he wouldn't have shot you anyway. He was as scared as you were."

"That's exactly why he could have!"

"Well," Keith said, "at least you identified him. To the police."

"You don't understand," Quinn insisted. "We'd all be dead right now."

Later, she watched herself on the ten o'clock news, curious about how the surf-haired reporter from Channel 3 had fashioned the story. The segment was called "Carjacker Gets Schooled." As it turned out, she was on for only about five seconds, gibbering about how frightened she'd been. Everything she'd said about Delaney—her bravery and heroism, the fact that she'd saved them from certain death—had been cut in favor of Green Boy's waggish account of the carjacker's stupidity. Delaney herself wasn't featured at all. Clearly, they were playing the story for laughs. It amazed Quinn that her own death could be consigned so easily to the ridiculous.

Though the truly amazing thing, the one that surprised Quinn, was how the experience affected her anxiety. Rather than turn her into a blubbering wreck, it seemed to improve her condition. In the weeks that followed, she managed to grow less and less afraid of things, refusing to dwell on those ominous collocations—"dirty bomb," say, or "spinal meningitis"—that used to keep her up at night. Her therapist said she'd experienced a massive exposure that may have helped to defuse her sense of panic. "In vivo flooding," she called it. And that wasn't all, either. Quinn got started on her dissertation again, which she hadn't touched for months. She brewed coffee every morning and immediately hunched to her desk, avoiding the stacks of trashy magazines—*Surfer, Home Décor Buyer*—she'd taken to reading on the couch. (What she'd wanted, and never found, was one called *Magazine Reader.*) Incredibly, she even went back to driving school. She found a more expensive class in the Richmond District and discovered that she could make a left turn or edge into a lane of traffic without freezing into a corpse. The instructor commended her boldness. Whenever she grew nervous or frightened, she'd think of Delaney's fingers squeezing her hand, a grip of invincible calm.

The rest of the time she spent as before, feeding her cat, Hitchcock, or sleuthing through back issues of *Artforum,* mulling over the pictures of dead-fly mosaics or people ducttaped to the wall or hotel rooms covered in Cheez Whiz. She was supposed to like this art. It was witty, no doubt about it, so why did she often feel—visiting a much-hyped show at SFMOMA—that the artist was crouched mischievously behind her, taping a KICK ME sign to her ass? It was exhausting, this type of cleverness. Sometimes Quinn felt the same weariness around her friends: their conversations seemed like a talent contest, a grinning rivalry of jokes. Of course, Quinn was as guilty as anyone. She'd come home from a party sometimes and try to remember the night's entertainment, wondering what on earth she'd talked about. It was during these moments—alone at 2:00 a.m., changing Hitchcock's litter in a fog of wine—that she felt the depth of her loneliness.

After a month or so, Quinn called the original driving school and got Delaney's number. The least she could do—in gratitude or kindness—was take her out to dinner.

• • •

"Wow," Delaney said. "It's great that you're driving. I quit the lessons after what happened."

Quinn had picked her up at the BART station on Sixteenth and they were driving to the movies. It was Delaney's suggestion, a movie—Sunday was her only night off and she was dying to see one. (They had to see the early show, because a guy was taking her out dancing "after hours.") Ordinarily, Quinn had her friends over every Sunday for game night, a tradition they'd picked up in grad school, but she'd called them at the last minute to cancel.

Quinn glanced at Delaney as she drove, feeling frumpy in her old jeans and T-shirt. For her date, Delaney was wearing high heels and a skirt and a satin blouse, cut low across her bosom. Her bangs, which Quinn remembered as falling delinquently in her eyes, hung in two perfect corkscrews on either side of her forehead. She held the jean jacket in her lap, folded carefully as before.

"Is Rex your dog?" Quinn asked.

"What?"

"The dog on your jacket. I couldn't help noticing."

"Oh, God. You kidding? Somebody at Cedar House gave it to me. I'm not used to these San Francisco summers." Delaney laughed. Cedar House was the residential treatment center she'd told Quinn about. They'd found her a place in the Tenderloin and helped her get a job as a night clerk, making twelve bucks an hour. "You know, though, the picture reminds me of Sadie. My ex-husband's dog. I swear, he loved that thing more than me." Delaney told a story about her wedding, how it was a hundred and twelve degrees in the shade. This was in Tucson, Arizona. They'd had it in the backyard because her ex-husband was too cheap to get a church. What's more, he lets Sadie out during the ceremony and she starts to hyperventilate and get all feverish. They have to hold off the wedding so he can stand there in his tuxedo, cooling her off with a hose. "Can you imagine that? A dog being hosed down at your wedding?"

"How long were you married?" Quinn asked politely.

"Seven months. Big success." She smoothed the static from her skirt. "What about you? Are you married?"

"No."

"Boyfriend?"

"I just broke up with a woman. About two months ago."

Delaney blushed. "Sorry. I'm always inflicting my own prejudices."

"It's okay," Quinn said, relaxing. "I date men sometimes too." She smiled. "Her name's Natasha. We're still friends."

"What happened? Do you mind if I ask?"

Quinn shrugged; she often wondered the same thing herself. They'd go to a movie together, some weepy Hollywood romance that had gotten good reviews, and Natasha would spend the whole ride home ridiculing its premise or listing the product placements. Quinn would agree and play along, ashamed of the furry lump of well-being in the pit of her stomach. Once they'd gone to a documentary about a domestic violence shelter, one of the most devastating films Quinn had ever seen, and afterward Natasha had complained about the sound track. "I mean, what was that? *Porno's Greatest Hits*? Were they being ironic?"

Near the movie theater, Quinn circled for parking and eventually found something on Eddy Street. There was a man sitting on the sidewalk in front of them, a flourish of shit puddled beside him. His bare feet were barnacled with scabs.

"Do your boobs hang low?" he asked them cordially as she locked up the car.

"Yeah, I swing them to and fro," Delaney said, without missing a beat.

Quinn looked at her, startled. They walked on as if nothing

had happened. With her friends there was shame in these encounters, a leaky silence you had to walk off. "I remember that song," she said. "Jesus. How does the rest go?"

"Can you tie them in a knot, can you tie them in a bow. Can you throw them over your shoulder, like a continental soldier." Delaney recited it like a poem.

"That's right! I thought we were the only girls who sang that. What does it mean, anyway—a 'continental soldier'?"

"Beats me," Delaney said.

They both laughed, Delaney tossing her head back and letting out a drunk-sounding whoop, as if she were limboing under a pole. A woman walking ahead of them glanced back to look.

"I always thought that was an Oconomowoc thing," Quinn said.

"Still is, probably. I grew up in Waukesha."

Quinn grabbed her shoulder. "You're from Wisconsin?"

"Yep. Cheesehead through and through." She glanced at Quinn's hand on her shoulder, laughing. "You too, I guess?"

"Yes! When I was little. We moved to New York when I was ten." Embarrassed, Quinn dropped her hand from Delaney's shoulder. Why was she so excited? Quinn remembered the last time she'd visited Oconomowoc, taking a stroll around the lake after dinner and encountering a parade of upbeat strangers, one after another, each of them erupting into a cheerful "Hi!" when she passed. After the thirtieth "Hi," she was prepared to throttle someone. Keith claimed there was arsenic in the lake and they were all brain-damaged. And of course there was the issue of Quinn's grandfather, whom she cared for dearly but who spent much of his day grumbling about the "Coloreds" and their tasteless TV shows. Yet this was the same place she'd loved as a child, the same blue lake that figured in her dreams. She used to spend hours swimming with her best friend, a chubby girl whose father was a minister. They'd splash each other from rafts and sing about low-hanging boobs until they were hoarse. Then they'd sit on the diving platform in the sun, brushing the scent from each other's hair, Quinn's back turning to silk as the breeze made little cat's-paws on the water.

"I like to escape," Delaney said after the movie, a romantic comedy about a mayoral candidate who falls in love with a stripper, mistaking her for a reporter from *The New York Times*. In the end, he finds out her true identity and sacrifices his political career to be with her. "I mean, there's enough suffering in reality, right? At Cedar we have this Scale of Feeling, like from one to ten? Ten being the worst? If you're feeling a nine, you're supposed to do these exercises to get you back down to wherever. Five or six. It's part of our 'safety plan.'" She glanced around the Starbucks they were in, clutching her coffee cup with both hands. Delaney had chosen the Starbucks: Quinn tried to relax to the Ella Fitzgerald oozing from the ceiling, worried that one of her friends might wander by in a FUCK CORPORATE COFFEE T-shirt. "Sounds corny, but movies do that for me."

"I liked it," Quinn said. "Really."

Delaney smiled. "You look a bit like that girl in the movie, what's her name? The main one? It's your glasses, I think."

"Unfortunately, mine are real. I've had them since I was six." She took off her glasses and groped around like a zombie.

"Can't be that bad, is it?"

"Blind as Monet," she said, frowning after the words had left her mouth. She felt like explaining herself, but the mere thought of the old sentimentalist, finishing his *Nymphéas* in near darkness, terrified her. What did it mean that they were his best paintings? "Actually, not blind. But I have this phobia? I'm scared to death of it. Like my vision will keep getting worse and then just go out like a TV set."

Delaney's eyes softened. "Catastrophic thinking. We learned techniques for that, too."

"When we moved to New York, these boys at my school— the Linehan twins—used to steal my glasses and hide them in the boys' bathroom. I couldn't see a thing. I'd have to fish them out of the urinal sometimes, on my hands and knees. Everyone called me Piss-Quinn from Wisconsin." She laughed. "I used to cry every night and ask my mom when we were moving back to Oconomowoc."

It was supposed to be nothing, a silly story, but Delaney grabbed her hand and held it on the table. Quinn felt the warmth of her fingers, a stillness like relief. "Is that where the blindness thing comes from?"

"Who knows? My therapist thinks it's a fear of death."

"I've got a fear of graveyards." Delaney told her a story about driving drunk one afternoon in Tucson with her ex-husband's retriever and running off the road into a saguaro cactus. She was wandering back to the road, in a daze, when she found this beautiful-looking cross nailed all over with bottle caps. An altar. "I had this weird feeling, like I'd found my own grave. There were these offerings too, like flowers and things? Even a tequila bottle." Delaney smiled, as if she were telling a happy story. "Sadie got thrown right through the window. I found her with her neck broken, ten feet from the car."

"Jesus," Quinn said.

"That's why I wear this jacket. Sort of to remind me where I've been." Delaney let go of her hand, blushing. "Anyway, that's my share."

"Share?"

"Oh, sorry. Like when you share something personal."

Aside from therapy, Quinn wondered when the last time she'd shared something personal was. She peered at her watch, out of habit. "Aren't you going to miss your date?"

Delaney dropped her eyes. When she looked up again, her face was shy and penitent. "I don't really have a date tonight. I just felt like getting dressed up." She glanced at the person sitting next to them, a girl with shredded jeans and an ellipsis of pebblelike studs over one eyebrow. "To be honest, with Cedar House and everything, it's been a long time since I've been out at all."

Quinn looked at her. Her hair was messed up from the wind outside, the perfect corkscrews sagging into peyos. Why did Quinn have such an urge to brush it? She imagined them watching a video together, another movie about the wacky imperialism of hope, while Quinn worked the day's tangles from her hair. She felt so comfortable around this overdressed woman that it didn't seem implausible. In fact, she wanted to ask Delaney over next weekend. But they barely knew each other, and Quinn was worried she'd misconstrue it as a date.

"Listen," she said, when they'd finished their coffees. "I have this thing on Sundays, with my friends. We go out to eat somewhere and then play these stupid games at my place. I could buy you dinner. Will you join us next week?"

The following Sunday, hoping to put Delaney at ease, Quinn got more dressed up than usual, wearing her favorite skirt and a silk, draped-neck shell she'd bought for special occasions. She was startled to see Delaney at the BART station wearing jeans and a pullover. She wore heels below her jeans, like a concession to her former elegance.

At the restaurant, Quinn introduced Delaney to her friends, who were already seated at a table. Natasha was there, and Quinn's friends Farid and Hershel—both from grad school. Keith sat at the far end of the table with his brilliant girlfriend Geetha, a string theorist preparing to do a postdoc at Princeton.

Quinn had tried to ask her about her area of study once, but she'd spent the whole time complaining about "flop transitions" and the "Theory of Everything." ("Well, it does have a nice ring to it," Quinn had said.) Delaney smiled at each person, greeting them carefully before sitting down. It depressed Quinn that all her friends were academics. To break the ice, she told them about the song she and Delaney had remembered last week; Quinn did her best to describe the lyrics, explaining how they couldn't figure out what a "continental soldier" was. No one knew what she was talking about and she was forced to sing it, energetically, to the table. Everyone looked at her breasts.

"Wow," Farid said.

"Talk about shock and awe," Natasha said.

A waiter came by and passed out menus. Geetha leaned forward and gave specific recommendations: the owner was a friend of her family's, a Rajasthani man with a surly temper. If you didn't eat everything on your plate, he took it as a personal insult and claimed Americans were spoiled.

"And yet he seems very patriotic," Hershel said. There was a sticker on the window next to him that said AMERICA: OPEN FOR BUSINESS.

Farid scowled. "America: Shut up and buy shit."

"I think it's great that everyone has flags up," Delaney said, apparently not hearing him. "Not that I agree with everything we're doing, politically, but it's really brought the country together."

There was an awkward silence. While they were waiting for their food, Quinn told the story of the carjacking though everyone had heard it before. It was a great story, and people laughed, but Quinn didn't know how to convey the intimacy of Delaney's valor—it was just an anecdote, like the farcical piece on Channel 3. How quickly everything got destroyed, rubbled into words. She put her hand on Delaney's back, and everyone raised their glasses in an impromptu toast. Delaney stared into her Coke, blushing at the attention.

"Did they ever find him?" Farid asked. "The carjacker?"

"Nope. Vanished."

Delaney looked up from her glass. "He was no professional, I'll tell you that much. Didn't have the mind-set. I remember the first time I stole a fifth of vodka, before I was in recovery, how scared I was. My heart was going like crazy. By the end, though, I was sticking bottles up my shirt without batting an eye. I even stole from my friends—money, CDs, whatever I could pawn."

"That's hard to believe," Quinn said, a little shocked. She wanted to steer the conversation back to Delaney's heroism.

"Oh, yeah. Once I stole from my own sister. She had this brass shoe—you know, like you make for your baby? My niece's! I couldn't even sell it, which is the disgraceful part."

Everyone stared at Delaney with subdued respect, more impressed by this than by the story of her bravery. Hershel started telling an anecdote about his ex-girlfriend, a choreographer from New York. They were supposed to move out here together, but she'd fallen in love with a forty-year-old sculptor at an artists' retreat in Vermont. Hershel was so furious he'd stolen her Egyptian bead necklace when he was packing up to leave. She'd inherited it from her grandmother. At the time it felt like revenge, but now—three years later—he was starting to feel guilty. It was worth a lot of money, and he felt like he should give it back.

"You're shoulding all over yourself," Delaney said.

Hershel looked at her, startled. "What?"

"Should this. Should that. You're forgetting about the three most important people in your life."

"I am?"

"Me, myself, and I. I used to be like that too. Trying to please everyone else. That's why I started drinking so much—I thought I didn't matter, I was worthless, and then I really *was* a monster to everyone. That's the ironical part."

"Maybe you're right," Hershel said, considering.

When the food came, Delaney peered at the dish of saag paneer in front of her, a look of pensive apprehension on her face. Quinn realized that she'd never had Indian food before. She was nervous about impressing them: why else would she be talking so much? Quinn touched Delaney's shoulder, doing her best to explain what each of the dishes were. "And that's bread," she said, pointing at the buttery mound of nan. "Delicious."

Delaney nodded. She pointed at Quinn's glass like a Hollywood Indian, her face stark and serious. "Water. Refreshing."

She threw her head back and laughed. Quinn blushed. While they ate dinner, Hershel and Natasha started to make fun of different teachers—art history professors—in their program. Delaney followed the conversation with interest, her eyes drifting to Hershel's beer whenever he topped off his glass. Quinn fidgeted in her chair, worried that she was going to bring up Jim Davis. Instead, she cleared her throat gently and asked the three of them what their favorite pieces of art were. If some aliens came down to Earth and you could show them one masterpiece, what would it be?

Hershel grimaced. "You mean to convince them not to destroy us?"

"Don't ask me," Natasha said. "I hate art."

Quinn realized they were too afraid of the question to answer it seriously. They turned to Quinn, waiting. She thought of an Eva Hesse sculpture, *Accession II*. From the outside, it seemed like an ordinary steel box, but when you peered inside it was grim and creaturely, brambled with metal thorns. To Quinn, it seemed like a perfect expression of grief. When she imagined showing it to the aliens, though, she couldn't get past the name without feeling like a fraud. It seemed incredibly pretentious. They'd take one look and zap her on the spot. Quinn glanced up from her plate and imagined Delaney as her judge, a Martian ambassador, waiting to be convinced that her life on Earth was worth living.

"I'll have to think about it," she said.

After dinner, they all went back to Quinn's place for a round of Fictionary. Quinn handed out pens and everyone sat Montessori-style on the floor—everyone, that is, except for Delaney, who perched uncomfortably on the edge of the sofa, as if she were on a witness stand. She held her seltzer with two hands, staring at the *Webster's International* stationed on the floor. Quinn sat beside her and explained the rules carefully, how one person chose a word no one knew and then everyone else made up a definition for it. Then they mixed all the definitions together and you had to guess which was the real one.

"Sounds fun," Delaney said, eyeing the Merlot in Natasha's glass.

Quinn was drinking a seltzer as well, in solidarity—but now she wished she hadn't served wine at all. They played a practice round while Delaney watched, Quinn sliding off the couch and joining the others on the floor. The word was "tohunga." As always, there were a number of geographically inspired entries: *a Polynesian water god with webbed feet, a Ugandan stew made from ostrich stock.* And of course the requisite throwaway—*the irresistible urge to stroll through Brooklyn, New York*—which caused the group to moan and throw their pens at Hershel, the suspected culprit. In the commotion Quinn glanced at Delaney, who sat there politely without laughing.

"It's a Maori priest," Farid said, announcing the real definition. "All the best men end up in the church."

Keith chose a word next: "carphophis." Delaney asked him to repeat the word, as if she might recognize it the second time around. Everyone wrote down their definitions and then handed them, one by one, to Keith. He read the definitions in a gravely pompous voice, looking directly at Quinn before reciting hers to the group: *a nervous condition of the scalp suffered by urban motorists*. Keith glanced at the next card and started laughing before he could stop himself. "A Dutch Danish," he said finally. There was giggling. Natasha scowled at Hershel, who held up his hands to show he wasn't responsible.

"Is that like a German chocolate cake from Iran?" Geetha said.

"More like a Spanish rice from Detroit."

Quinn glanced at Delaney, who was staring at her lap with an embarrassed look. It suddenly occurred to Quinn that this game—the whole evening, in fact—was a mistake. It was hot and airless in the apartment, and she began to feel a straitening of dread, like a seat belt cinched across her chest. When they went around the circle to cast their votes, she pretended to think about it and eventually guessed "a Dutch Danish" without looking at the couch.

"You don't need to help me," Delaney said to her, after the real definition was announced. "Mine was the stupidest one."

"What? No. You get a point for tricking me."

On Delaney's turn to pick a word, she opened the huge dictionary and studied it for a long time before choosing "paroxysm," pronouncing each syllable as if they were individual words in a sentence. Quinn's heart sank. Everyone smiled awkwardly and wrote down their definitions. When it came time to guess the real one, however, they all picked "a sudden attack or spasm." Quinn thought about choosing one of the fake definitions, but it would be too conspicuous and she didn't want to push her luck. Also, frankly, she didn't want her friends to think she didn't know the meaning.

"You all knew that word," Delaney said.

Natasha smiled apologetically. "Years of therapy. I wouldn't have known except for 'paroxysm of guilt.'"

"SAT word," Farid said, then looked embarrassed.

Delaney stood up from the couch and put her drink on the mantel. "Play the next one without me. I'm just going out for a smoke."

She sidestepped around the circle and clicked across the room, almost walking into the closet before finding the front door. Everyone sat there without speaking. Quinn wondered if she should follow Delaney outside and apologize, but couldn't figure out what she would say. She felt sick to her stomach. The phone rang, a diversion, and she went into the kitchen to answer it. It was the Indian restaurant, the owner. His voice was curt and peevish. There'd been some mistake: they'd left without paying. That's impossible, Quinn said. The owner said it was unfortunately quite possible and they weren't always lucky enough to have the customer's phone number. She asked if he was absolutely sure. Yes, they'd discovered it right away and left a message an hour ago. Quinn hung up the phone and looked at her answering machine, surprised to see the green light actually blinking.

"We left ninety-eight dollars," Keith said. "I counted it myself."

"Maybe the guy's lying? Was he angry at us?"

"I left a bone on my plate," Natasha lamented. "I should have eaten everything."

Farid stood up. "We definitely paid. Maybe the waiter nabbed it."

A feeling passed through Quinn, a jolt of recognition—like

when you're flying through a patch of turbulence and see the fear, the normally imperceptible truth, on a stranger's face. She felt a strange jag of relief. She looked up. Everyone seemed to read her thoughts: they glanced toward the door, their faces grave and bashful.

Quinn rushed down to the lobby and pushed through the heavy door, peering out at the empty sidewalk. Too late: she was gone. A plastic bag tumbleweeded down the street. There was a liquor store on the next block, and Quinn thought about running there and checking the aisles. She turned back in sadness and saw Delaney sitting against the wall of the building, squinting at her through a twirl of smoke, like a hardened thief.

"The restaurant called," she said, trying to control her voice. "They say we never paid them."

Delaney regarded her carefully. Quinn could feel herself trembling. Her heart was racing; she knew she must look wild, frantic. A drunken laugh drifted from a fire escape somewhere above them. Delaney's face began to change, flushing red before congealing into an angry mask.

"Oh, I get it." She stood up and lifted her chin, nostrils winged in defiance. She jerked her head toward the building. "Did they send you out here?"

"No," Quinn said. "It was my idea."

"I'm going to get my coat."

Quinn watched her try the door unsuccessfully before searching the long column of doorbells for the right button to push. The door buzzed after a minute and Quinn followed her inside. Delaney's feet clacked up the stairs, a flight ahead of Quinn's. She almost slipped on the first landing, grabbing the banister at the last moment to catch herself. Suddenly, Quinn wished she'd never told anyone about the phone call, wished she'd just agreed to pay the restaurant herself. She imagined the angry mob upstairs, a swarm of Signorelli demons, seizing Delaney and tearing through her pockets. When she reached the top of the stairs, though, Quinn's friends were gathered peacefully in the cramped hallway, their heads slumped in silence. They refused to look at Delaney, who was standing right in front of them.

"You won't believe this," Keith said with a sheepish grin, baring his wallet and revealing a wad of bills. "After counting it, I guess I just stuck it in my wallet. The whole stack! We were talking about the A's versus the Giants. I must have been on another planet."

Quinn drove back to the BART station, the old *Jaws*-y panic returning unexpectedly, like a magic spell being lifted. Her palms stuck to the steering wheel, sweating in a way she'd forgotten about. She crossed Twenty-fourth Street and then back-tracked around the block to avoid making a left turn. Delaney kept her eyes fixed ahead of her, as if she were reading something of great importance on the windshield. She hadn't spoken to Quinn since the apartment. If she noticed the fear in Quinn's eyes, that they were driving more slowly than before, she didn't so much as glance at her face.

They passed a mural on St. Peter's Church. The garish use of color depressed Quinn, and she remembered what her favorite piece of art was. It was a painting, a nearly anonymous Van Gogh. She couldn't even remember the title—only that it was a landscape, painted before he moved to France and discovered color. The painting was of a house, a rural cottage, its thatched roof darkening while the sky around it cooled to dusk. In the foreground was a woman with her back turned. She was trapped outside in the windy weather, peering in at a speck of fire in the house, as if she'd wandered by and was remembering the warmth of her childhood.

"Why did you save my life?"

Delaney stared at the street. Music lurched from the bars on Twenty-fourth Street, rowdy and polkalike. "I don't know," she said, shrugging.

"Probably you're wondering why you ever did. I wouldn't blame you if you were." Quinn laughed, miserably. "I was just curious if you . . . I don't know. Had a reason."

Delaney kept her eyes on the windshield. Creeping in second gear, Quinn drove past a man soliloquizing on the corner in a rumpled suit and aviator glasses, like an FBI agent on a bender. He was holding a sign that said THE PLANETS ARE CRYING AND YOU'RE TOO WEAK TO HEAR THEM. He stopped speaking and his face followed Quinn, slow and puppetlike, as if he were divining the terrors in her soul. A fear of sorrowful planets. A fear of loneliness when paying the bills. A fear of triteness, of corny honest words, that made her heart small and safe and driven to the dark.

"You're a human being, right?"

Quinn looked at herself in the rearview mirror: an involuntary glance. They stopped at a red light near the BART station and waited in silence. Quinn would drop her off at the next corner—good-bye, a wretched wave—and that would be it. In all likelihood, they'd never see each other again. Delaney turned suddenly and looked at Quinn for the first time, leaning toward her in the glow of the streetlights. Her face was strange and serious. She reached up and took off Quinn's glasses, tenderly, tilting them from her ears like a lover. Quinn was astonished. She hadn't realized how much she'd wanted this, to be kissed. And Delaney wanted it too? Enough to forgive her? Her breath warmed Quinn's face as she folded the glasses. Quinn closed her eyes and waited, heart pounding in her chest.

The door slammed—a noise like a shot—and Quinn opened her eyes. She couldn't see anything. It was all a blur. She tried to focus on the street, baffled by the smear of colors. She squinted at the red nova of the traffic light. The nova turned green and cars began to honk. Quinn gripped the wheel, helplessly. She would have to move. To drive. Maybe Delaney would come back? She crouched there, praying, while people began to yell from their cars, calling her terrible things.

Animals Here Below

WE HAVEN'T SEEN OUR MOTHER in really long, a long time, three years almost, so when she pulls up to the curb and gets out of her station wagon, Caitlin and I run out there to touch her hair. It's the longest hair I've ever seen, blond and slithery and down to her rear. My mom laughs and bends over and lets us feel how heavy it is. Mr. Grown-Up, she calls me. We fill our arms with hair, which smells like French fries. So long, it makes me want to not let go.

I make up a song, because that's what I always do. *Hair of Ages, who do you trust? Hair of Ages, taller than us.*

Dad doesn't come out to see her hair. We used to be rich, but now my father works at the airport handling people's luggage. A ramp agent, he's called. He's got these coveralls that say HUDSON GENERAL on them and plastic earmuffs that look like headphones. He wears them at the kitchen table sometimes, when Caitlin and I talk about our mother. If she hadn't fallen in love with the math teacher, none of this would have happened. Now she's back from Alaska. If I ask Dad about it, he just laughs for no reason and says: "I guess she's fed up with him, too."

My mom follows us into the kitchen, glancing around the house and stopping now and then to shake her head. She's never been here before. I keep sneaking glances at her face. She's paler than I remember, and you can see right through her eyebrows to the skin underneath. When she smiles, secret lines crease out from the corners of her mouth, three or four on each side, like ripples getting smaller.

Caitlin's gone Special Ed and just keeps staring at her, mouth unhinged. She's six and doesn't know she's being rude. There's a sugar crust of sleep in her eyelashes.

"I have some presents for you in the car," Mom says, leaning her head to one side and swinging her hair around to the front, slow and gentle, like a crane moving something heavy. She peers at the door to my dad's room, where he's pretending to be asleep. It's only recently they've begun talking again. She was going to stay at a hotel, but I got Caitlin to throw one of her tragic fits.

"Tomorrow night we can see a movie," Caitlin says, too loudly.

Mom blushes pink, right through her eyebrows. "Your father didn't tell you? I can only stay for a night."

"Why?" I say. Dad did tell us, but this is part of our plan. Mine and Caitlin's.

"I have an interview in Austin. At a school there. They need someone to teach music." She squats down to our height. "But I'll come back to Tucson in a couple weeks to visit, after I get settled at your aunt Tina's."

"We're not going to the Desert Museum?"

She studies me carefully. "Yes, in the morning. I promised we would."

She asks for some water and I get her a glass down from the cupboard, inspecting the rim for little orange juice bits. Then I open the freezer for some ice before remembering what's in there. Zoomer, our cocker spaniel, died last week from dog cancer, and my dad plans to send him to a renderer in Montana who does museum skeletons. Supposedly, the guy has some special bugs that are going to clean Zoomer's skull, make it shiny and beautiful, something you can put on your desk. Dermestid beetles, they're called. It's giving Caitlin nightmares and I have to sing her a song about good beetles that don't eat your face off. *Pretty beetle, he sleeps in the wind. Nibbles grass but never your skin.*

Zoomer gives me a sad look through his plastic bag, little icicles dangling from his beard. "Bad dog," I mouth. The renderer's on vacation, which is why Zoomer's in the freezer, but I wonder if my dad's trying to do everything possible to make my mother run away again.

I hand her the ice water, worried it smells like dog, but she doesn't notice and takes a long drink. The ice ticks against the glass, even when she's finished. She goes over to the window and looks at our backyard, which is just a dirt place surrounded by a chain-link fence, the only thing of interest being a clothes wire stretched tight with a little crank, my dad's blue jeans walking in the wind. Something about Mom's looking at it in her fancy sandals makes me feel ashamed.

She plucks at the back of her dress, which is dark down the middle. "I forgot it could get like this."

"It's monsoon season," Caitlin says.

"She knows!" I tell her.

Caitlin looks like she might cry, the little scar on her cheek dimpling into a V. My mom used to help me search for monsoons when I was younger, casing the sky with binoculars. That was before she ran off with Mr. Osterhout, when we lived in a big house with air-conditioning and a view of the mountains and javelinas that drowned in the pool if you didn't close the gate. The mountains were covered in saguaro cactus, which could kill you if they fell over but they never did. At night the wind went through them and they sounded like music. Mom used to take us out there before bed, me and Caitlin and sometimes my dad, and we'd listen to the cactus humming everywhere at once, some of them two hundred years old and taller than our house. She knew exactly what letter it was in, C or B flat. My dad called her Miss Solemnis, after her favorite Beethoven song.

After she left, though, everything changed. Dad stopped going to work so he could listen to her CDs all day long, the same ones he'd always thought were boring. He'd drive us to school in his bathrobe and then pick us up as if no day had gone by, the hairs on his chest sticking out for everyone to see. He'd never paid much attention to Zoomer before, but then he started buying dog groceries every day, feeding him pigs' ears and chicken croissants and K-9 Kupcakes. Zoomer even began sleeping in bed with him. They'd snuggle together, refusing to get up before noon. After he got fired from the bank, I stopped at my dad's door in the middle of the day and he was lying there with his eyes closed, letting Zoomer lick his toes. I watched Zoomer clean every toe like a cat, one through ten.

That was the "lower depths," as my dad calls it. I thought he'd escaped them, but now he hasn't been to work at all since Zoomer died and even made me call the airport yesterday to tell them he had bronchitis.

Mom takes me and Caitlin outside again to her station wagon, which is filled with shoes and boxes and garbage bags tied into mouse ears at the tops. The desert sun squinches her eyes. She hands us presents, wrapped up carefully with red ribbons, like the ones she sends from Alaska. I rip off the paper and pull out a box filled with little totem poles, which she explains is a chess set made of whalebone. I don't even know how to play chess, but I pretend to love it anyway because of the plan. We're going to make our mom fall in love with us again. With our father, too, even. That way she'll stay here forever and he'll stop being depressed and we'll be in the higher depths like we used to, moving back to the mountains where we can hear the cactus.

"I brought Zoomer something too," she says, holding up a fake bone with the words TOP DOG written on it. "Where is he, anyway?"

"Dog heaven," Caitlin says sadly.

I give her a dirty look, because she's forgotten what we agreed to say. "It's a dog kennel," I explain. "He's not dead."

Mom squints at me, one hand cupped above her eyes. "Why is he at the kennel?"

"It's a school. They're training him to be obedient."

I say this since I'm on the spot and Dad used to joke about sending Zoomer to Regurgitation Training because there was so much dog puke cookied to the rug. Mom seems not to remember this. Luckily, the screen door squeaks into a slam and my father appears on the porch, wearing his Hudson General cap and flip-flops. He flops over to us. There's a pearl of shaving cream perched on the rim of his glasses. He stares at my mom's hair, like someone in a trance. She looks down at her feet and hands him the fake bone she bought for Zoomer. Her face is all shy and speechless, and for a minute I think the plan's working before we've really started.

Dad puts the bone in his teeth, I guess for a joke. No one says anything. He blushes and takes it out of his mouth.

"Nice to be back on top," he says, reading the words on it.

My mom's face hardens. "Don't start."

"Hoo, boy. Started." He peers in the window of the station

wagon, then looks out at the trash-filled street. "Take your stuff in for the night. This isn't Via Roma Road."

While my mom showers for dinner, Caitlin and I run off to our room to put away our presents. The sound of water moans from the wall. I put the chess set on my dresser, which is already covered in gifts. There's the creepy-looking spirit mask, the pouch containing real live gold dust, the erasable globe where you're supposed to write in the country names like a test. I spin the globe to make sure you can see the little drawing on it, the stick-figure woman standing where Alaska should be, which my mom must have Magic Markered in herself. The woman is smiling, holding a harpoon in one hand. Once my dad got drunk and wrote WHORE underneath the drawing when I was asleep. In the morning he looked very ashamed and even started crying when he erased it.

Caitlin and I put our ears to the wall and listen to Mom's voice, which is singing through the hum of pipes. The words are in a different language, long and beautiful. While we're waiting, I take down the shoe box from the closet and pull out my favorite letter. The envelope has the stamp of a moose on it, pasted next to a black circle that says FAIRBANKS AK around the edge. I open the letter carefully, because it's tearing at the folds.

Dear kids,

A few days ago we saw the first aurora borealis, which are these swirling green lights up in the sky. They're kind of like a gigantic moving curtain. You know when people say "breathtaking"? They actually took my breath. I wish you'd been here to see them. Maybe soon, when we find our own place, you can come up to visit. Ian, you'd get a kick out of Matt's brother. He has a big red beard and breeds sled dogs, which he keeps outside even in the rain. They're the best behaved dogs in the world (nothing like Zoomer!). You tell them to stay, just like that, and they don't move for as long as you can watch.

None of the schools here need music teachers, so I've been keeping at home while Matt teaches. I'm trying to prepare myself for the all-day darkness. Sometimes I think about your real mother and get jealous and upset because she could have taken you with her. But I can't, your dad would never let me.

Other times I think about things I want to say to you and send them to you in my head. I even close my eyes. Matt's brother has this tape, about mind reading. It says you're supposed to picture your thoughts like snowballs. You're supposed to pack them really tight, I guess to make you concentrate. Crazy, I know. Once in a while I'll hear one of your voices in my head, saying hello Mom or are you happy, and I wonder if you're sending me snowballs too.

XOXO
Mom

Caitlin asks me to read it out loud again and I do, skipping the lines about our real mother, who died in the hospital when she was born. Afterward, we sit on the bed and choose a message to send with our brains. A single word, to make it easy. Then we close our eyes and beam it at Mom in the bathroom, packing the word into a snowball, a hard and shiny secret. *Stay.*

Later, she asks us to help with her hair, which looks brown and seaweedy from the shower. Caitlin and I take turns with the dryer, trying to make her hair as nice as possible for our father. It shimmers under the hotness and turns blond again. "Va Va Va Bloom!" Caitlin shouts, pushing her into our room.

This is the name of the lipstick we picked out. We bought it yesterday at Walgreens, while Dad was shopping for garbage bags. My mom looks at her suspiciously but tries the lipstick, puckering her lips at the mirror above the bed, which makes me think maybe she heard our thoughts through the wall.

She unpuckers her lips when she sees all the presents on my dresser. For a minute, her face looks frozen. "I forgot about drawing that," she says finally, staring at the smiley-faced woman clutching her harpoon. "Did you think of me like that?"

I nod, hoping it will make her happy. She looks out the window. I want to ask her about the aurora borealis, or the sled dogs in the rain, but something in her face makes me think twice.

"Does Fairbanks get below zero?" I ask. The idea seems incredible.

She frowns, turning the globe so we can't see Alaska. "You know how cold it is? No one can turn their engines off. They just leave them running in the parking lot, like a humongous smog machine."

While we're waiting for the pizza guy to show up with dinner, Caitlin and I go to find my father, who's lying in bed and reading his favorite book, *Strange but True Dog Tales*. He takes off his plastic earmuffs. We have to lie and say that Mom begged him to join us. Even then, he shows up at the table with his book, barely glancing at her lips before going back to whatever he was reading.

"Listen to this," he says. "'The faithful dog Hachiko, from Tokyo, Japan, was famously attached to his master, Professor Eisaburo Uyeno. Each day, "Hachi" would accompany Professor Uyeno to the train station when he left for work and meet him there, tail wagging, upon his return.'" My dad reads how Professor Uyeno died at work one day and Hachi went to the station like always, waiting for him to come back. He did this for more than ten years. Finally Hachi died too, in the same spot he'd last seen his friend alive. When he gets to this part, my dad's eyes mist up, though he's read this story to us before. He seems to have chosen it on purpose. "Incredible. They've put up a statue of him in the train station."

Mom glares at him, her eyes not misted at all. "Is this how you entertain the children?"

"What?" he says. "They love these stories."

"No, we don't," I say. The lie makes me fidget.

My father looks at me, betrayed. He frowns at Caitlin and then back at me. "What about Daisy, the poodle with psychic powers?"

I look down at the table. Caitlin starts blowing bubbles in her milk, which she does when she's nervous. "Mom has ESP," she says. "She can hear our thoughts."

Dad blinks at my mother, who blushes pink again. She stares at her lap. "It's nothing. Just something I feel sometimes."

"Your mother does not have ESP," he says. "That's ridiculous."

My dad goes back to his book but keeps glancing up at the three of us, as though he's jealous of something. When the pizza comes, he insists on saying grace. "Praise God from whom all blessings flow," he says, "praise God all animals here below." Instead of saying amen, he and Caitlin bark into their pressed-together hands. It started out as a joke, but since Zoomer died we've been doing it every night like a religious event.

My mom scrapes her chair. "Is this normal behavior around here?"

"Maybe you have a better prayer," my dad mumbles. "About logarithms."

"What?"

"I'm sorry. I promised." He looks at the dog bowl in the corner, his voice catching in his throat. "I just miss Zoomer, is all. I keep waiting for him to start whimpering and paw my lap."

"Logarithms are covered in ants," I sing. *"Throw them in the fire, dance dance dance."*

"Why don't you just go and get him?" Mom says, ignoring me.

"What?"

"Zoomer! From Dog Heaven! Go there and bring him home?"

Dad stares at her in disbelief. "Just whip up there myself?"

"Sure," she says, shrugging. "If you miss him so much."

"Christ, Jane. Do you think I wouldn't?"

"What? Has he been biting other dogs?"

"How in God's name would I know?" Dad whispers.

He puts his face in his hands. After a minute he gets up and grabs Zoomer's bowl before trudging back to his room. This is not how we've planned things. My dad used to make us laugh all the time, but now he cries at the table for no reason. Last month, at the airport, he saw a man die. Another ramp agent. The guy stepped too close to the engine of a 747 and flew head-first into it, like Superman. I wish I could tell this story to Mom, because it might help her understand something. A pepperoni's hanging from the slice of pizza in her hand, caught in a cheese-slide to her plate.

"He's sad because of you," I tell her, glancing at Caitlin. "If you stayed here, longer, it would help him."

"Oh, Ian." My mom sighs, napkining her lipstick. "I'm not the sort of help he needs."

In the middle of the night, I get Caitlin up and we slip from our beds, tiptoeing through the TV room where my mom sleeps on the foldout couch. This is part two of our plan. We sneak into the kitchen and I go through the knife drawer, testing the tips. Insects buzz all around us, like static. Caitlin's too nervous to speak. Quietly, I open the freezer and check on Zoomer, who's grown another icicle. I ask him if we're being bad dogs. He doesn't answer me, only looks.

"I'm *not* a dog," Caitlin whispers.

In the daylight, you can see the stabs in the rubber, pushed out like lips. There's one on each tire, which have sunk down to the hubcaps. Dad circles the car in his robe. A wishbone of veins bulges from his temple. He eyes me and Caitlin, who's squatting in the yard and plucking at some weeds. For some reason, she's covering the scar on her cheek.

"I don't believe this," Mom says. She sits on the hood, pinching the wedge of nose between her eyes. "I just put new tires on."

I'm worried Caitlin might say something, but she's too busy killing weeds. A homeless guy walks by on the other side of the street, pushing his shopping cart up the sidewalk and yelling at the lady in front of him, who's riding an electric wheelchair. "Fucking cunt!" he yells. "I told you that from the first beginning!" My mom glares at my father, as though the bad words are his fault.

"Sunday in the neighborhood," she says.

"Hell," Dad says, still looking at the tires. He squints down the road. "I don't know what's going to be open."

One place, it turns out, but it's in South Tucson and my dad can't get anyone at the tire shop who speaks English. Mom calls our aunt Tina in Texas, her voice taut and whispery. Still, the plan works out even better than we thought, because she can't drive a stick shift and my father has to take the four of us to the Desert Museum in our Blazer. There's some dog fur on the passenger seat, and Mom brushes it into a little tumbleweed and sticks it in the ashtray before sitting down. She has to sit on her hair, because the air-conditioning's going full blast. It smells like zombie breath. (Some rats were living in the engine for a while and never got out.) Amazingly, my dad has on a fancy-looking shirt with a little button at the back of the collar, which I haven't seen him wear since he was senior loan officer at the bank. His hair is combed back, parted straight as a pencil. Caitlin and I watch him in the rearview mirror. He keeps his eyes on the road, glancing now and then at the dog hair in the ashtray.

We leave the haze of the city and drive toward the mountains, which from a distance look as barren as the moon. When we pass Bianchi's Pizza, the mountains suddenly go 3-D, cactus everywhere you look, their corduroy arms shimmering in the sun. It's like a see-through forest. Some of the cactus have white flowers blooming out the tops in Martian clumps. We wind up Gates Pass Road, driving by the scenic turnout where I used to set up kamikaze jumps for my bike.

"Can we look at the house?" I ask.

"No," Dad says.

Mom gives him a funny look. "You take them by the Via Roma house?"

"Sometimes." He coughs and meets my eyes in the rearview mirror. "If we're up here anyway."

Something sad drifts into my mom's face. She looks out the window, watching the street signs. "Does it look the same?"

"They've put in a hot tub. Where the deck used to be." Dad fiddles with the mirror. "It's good for the, um, javelinas. Speeds up the mating process."

Mom actually smiles. I catch Caitlin's eye and we sort of chuckle along in the backseat, even though I don't really get the punch line. How long has it been since he said something funny? I think up a song: *"Javelinas are mating, why aren't you? Javelinas in the hot tub, cook me a stew."*

"What on earth is that?" Mom asks, laughing. "A commercial?"

"A song!" Caitlin says ecstatically.

"My God. Where does he get that from?"

My dad frowns in the mirror. "Where do you think?"

At the Desert Museum, everyone stares at my mother's hair, as though it's one of the exhibits. It's so hot that the animals mostly shadow-bathe without moving. We look at the bighorn sheep, the coatis, the black bear lurking in its cave. I rush my dad past the Mexican wolf sleeping like roadkill, worried he might start thinking of Zoomer and get distracted. In Cat Canyon, the jaguarundi slumps on a rock and just sort of eyes us in a depressed way, and Dad says it's because all the jaguars say "Yo, jaguarundi!" whenever they see him. For the yo part, he uses a dopey Italian voice. This is the second joke in one day, a miracle, so Caitlin and I go spastic laughing and spend a long time trying to duplicate my dad's voice.

Mom laughs too, smiling her new wrinkles. All around us are families, normal ones with two parents, and it makes my heart jump ahead that we're the same as everyone else.

Outside the Hummingbird Aviary, my mom gets sort of quiet again and puts her hand on my head. This is my favorite part of the museum. There must be a thousand hummingbirds in one little place, which means they dart around you and hover at your face and zip past your ear like the letter Z in flight. It's scary and beautiful at the same time. The birds are all different colors, and you have to keep yourself from swatting them like flies. Mom barely makes it through the door before they swarm all around her, attracted to her hair. She closes her eyes and doesn't move an inch. They shoot around her head like sparks. Dad calls her the Bird Lady, and Caitlin and I take the end of her hair and stretch it as far as we can walk so that she laughs and does a curtsy. One of the hummingbirds actually lands on the bridge of hair we've made, still as a picture. It makes my breath stop moving, too.

On the drive back we barely talk, the sun burning through my shorts. My mom spots some coyotes in the road and touches my dad's leg. He brakes the car. The coyotes cross in front of us and saunter into some shrubs. Dad doesn't move. Mom keeps her hand there for a few seconds before snapping out of her trance.

"I do miss it here," she says.

When we get home, Dad checks the answering machine while Mom's in the bathroom. An old man's voice, deep and crackly. The skull doctor, he calls himself. He says he's back from vacation and to send Zoomer's head in for a "beetle bath." My dad looks embarrassed. I flash Caitlin a secret look.

"What a kook," Dad says, frowning. He slips into a TV voice: *"Beetles, take me away!"*

Later, after we've gone to bed, I can hear Mom and Dad talking in the kitchen. I'd forgotten what it sounded like, the deep and high responding to each other. It makes me feel safe and rich again. I nudge the top bunk with my foot, and Caitlin and I get up quietly and sneak down the dark hall to watch. Mom is sitting on the floor of the kitchen, my father crouched behind her in a chair. Her hair spills over his legs. He brushes it slowly, starting at the top of her head and following it down to the mess in his lap. Each stroke takes a long time. If he goes too fast, my mom turns stiff and bunches her shoulders. Caitlin stiffens along with her in the dark. Dad rests his arm between brushes and then starts again at the top. "What a pain in the hair," he says, his voice small and serious. "I always liked it short"; but it's more of a fact than a complaint, like maybe they'd be better off without it.

• • •

Though it's his day off, Dad actually gets up early the next morning to cook breakfast, his hair combed back again like a banker's. He makes Mom laugh by flipping pancakes at the ceiling. He even finds a garage for her where they speak English. Caitlin and I squeeze along in the tow truck with my mom, watching TV in the waiting room while her tires get changed. She checks her watch during commercials, craning her neck to peer into the garage, but after last night I'm not worried.

Through the window I can see a pack of clouds, inching in from the mountains, creeping like a spider on lightning legs. "A monsoon," I tell my mother, who bends close to the window to look.

"I love that smell," she says, closing her eyes.

"What smell?" Caitlin asks.

"Wet desert." Mom looks hushed and happy. "I forgot about it."

When we get home, I'm sweating from the storm in the air. Mom goes to change her clothes, and I slink into the kitchen and open the freezer to cool off. Empty. No Zoomer. Caitlin comes over and does a wide-eyed blink, because the plan's working even better than we thought. I stick my head inside, which feels like dog heaven.

I'm basking in the cold when my mother screams. A screech, like the squeal of a car.

I rush out to the backyard. She's standing on the porch and staring down at my father, who's kneeling over a dead dog in the dirt, the back of his BORN TO RUN T-shirt soaked with sweat. He has his earmuffs on and doesn't hear us. The tool in his hands whines through Zoomer's neck. Our battery-powered carving knife.

Just as the head slumps off, Dad notices us by the screen

door. He turns red and stands up quickly, carving knife hanging at his side. There's blood on his T-shirt, freckling Bruce Springsteen's face.

"You're back early," my father says, yanking the earmuffs to his neck. "I wasn't expecting you. For an hour." He looks at the head, which has rolled away from its body and is staring dead-faced at the sky, tongue tossed back like a scarf. "Took forever to melt. Zoom Zoom. He's finally thawed through." He's shaking, eyes pink and bleary. He bends down and picks up Zoomer's head, like a baseball. "I'm sending it to the skull doctor."

My mom just stands there. "What?"

"The renderer. He's preparing the skull. He only wants Zoomer's head."

She turns to me, white as her eyebrows.

"He has some beetles that'll eat off his face," I explain.

This doesn't seem to help. Caitlin starts to cry, staring at the headless Zoomer. Mom puts a hand over Caitlin's eyes and leads her into the kitchen. My dad stands in the yard for a minute, holding the head in front of him. He lays it on the porch with two hands and then follows my mom inside, trying to explain about Zoomer's cancer and how close they were before he died.

"So you've got the kids lying for you!" Mom stares at the wide-open door of the freezer. As if for the first time, she takes in the bubbled wallpaper and stove crusted with food before fastening on the sink, our dishes towered there from breakfast. Caitlin is still crying, a worm of snot peeking from her nose. "Look at this dump! It's no wonder they're traumatized. You can't even take care of yourself." My mom closes her eyes. "I should have seen this coming."

My dad's face looks sore, as though he's been slapped. "Right," he mumbles. "With your psychic powers."

"What?"

"ESP. Very convenient. You can skip off to Alaska and still talk to the kids every day."

"You're going to talk to me about raising kids!"

Dad smiles in an ugly way. He bows his head and puts his fingers to his temples, as though remembering a date. "Go ahead, psychic woman. Show us your powers. I'm thinking of a word."

"Don't, Howard. Jesus."

"It starts with *w*."

"We'll be normal," I say.

My mom covers her ears. "I should never have stayed here. I knew this was a mistake."

I grab her hair. I can't think of a song right away and so I pull it as far as it goes, like we did at the Desert Museum to make her laugh. "Ow!" she yells. "Ian, that hurts!" She rips her hair away from my hands. She goes into the TV room and shuts the door. I can hear her inside packing up her things.

Outside again, my dad digs a grave for Zoomer's body, which has started to draw flies. He mutters to himself as he works, the earmuffs still clamped around his neck. Afterward, he seals Zoomer's head in a garbage bag and lays it tenderly in a box, stuffing the top with Blue Ice packets. The box says FRAGILE on the side.

"Go get your sister," he tells me. He holds the box in the air. "We're going to the post office. Your mom wants to be alone."

"No," I say.

"She came all the way to see you. She won't sneak out before we get back."

He grabs my arm and I start to flail, making him drop the package with Zoomer's head in a prickly pear. My dad tightens his grip. When he speaks, though, his voice is calm and gentle.

"She was never going to live with us."

"Yes, she *was*."

"I'm sorry, kiddo. She was leaving today, anyway. You can slash her tires all you want." He loosens his grip. A fly sits on his wedding ring, like a jewel. "She gets sick inside, your mother. You don't realize that. It's all hooray-the-greatest for a while. Everything's 'breathtaking.' Like Alaska, I'm sure. Then suddenly she can't bear another minute."

His face looks weak. Weak and stupid, the earmuffs skewed around his neck. I yank my arm away and fish the box from the prickly pear and hold it in front of my face.

"Kiss me," I say like a woman. My voice is shaking.

"Stop it," he says.

"I'm still alive. Kiss me with your tongue."

"Stop it!"

"Hump me, big boy. I want your puppies."

I push the box at his face, making a kissing sound with my lips. My dad grabs it from my hands. I bolt away from him and run around the side of the house, my shoes slapping as they hit the driveway. "Dogfucker!" I shout. I want everyone to hear. I run into the front yard, which smells sweet and cindery in the first drops of rain. The drops make little craters in the dirt. After a while, my dad rounds the house and walks down the driveway, dragging Caitlin by the hand. The box with Zoomer's head is cradled under one arm. He looks at me for only a second—a sad sort of *who are you?*—before getting into the Blazer and backing out the drive.

I lie down in the dirt, closing my eyes. It starts to rain. To pour. It's like the sky just opens up and collapses. Rain pelts my eyelids, gurgling all around me. My shirt soaks through, painted to my skin. I can feel the ground melting beneath me. I can't breathe or talk or open my eyes. The rain nibbles at my face, eating it away speck by speck.

Unless my mother finds me. Unless she hears my thoughts

and runs out of the house and plucks me from the rain. *Help me,* I think, trying to pack the thought into a snowball. The ground is flooding. Water creeps up my neck, warm and bath-tubby. I wait and wait and wait. I beam more thoughts at my mother, picturing them like darts this time, flying through the window and bull's-eyeing her brain. Water seeps into my ears. The rain goes quiet, devouring my face. I want my mom to save me. I want to lie in bed with her, snuggled there till noon.

After a long time, the rain slows to a normal drip. Someone scoops me from the mud. It's not my mother. It's a strange man, lifting me by the armpits. His glasses are steamed into little moons. He shakes me till my ears unplug, sparkling inside from the leftover water.

"Are you okay?" he shouts.

I nod. My father sets me down. He clutches me tightly, as though I'm going to slip through his fingers. His nipples, strange and hairy, show through his T-shirt. For some reason, they make me feel alive. Caitlin lurks behind him in the rain, hugging the box with Zoomer's head.

"The streets are flooded!" she explains to our mother, who comes out with an umbrella. "We couldn't drive."

Mom shakes her head, staring at the box. The TV murmurs through the screen door. She looks old to me and tired, holding the umbrella with two hands. "For God's sake, you're soaked. Kids, get inside right now! You'll die of the flu."

"They'll be fine. It's the middle of the summer." Dad lets go of me. "They're stronger than I am."

She looks at his bloody shirt. "What are you? A doctor?"

"I'm their father," my dad says.

By afternoon the streets are still flooded, people getting swamped in the middle of the road. On TV, we see some rescuers pull an old man from his car, his shorts shoved up so you can see his diaper. My mom's garbage bags are lined up neatly by the door. Through the window I can see her sitting on the porch, staring out at our street, which has turned into a brown river like the others. She looks stiff and untouchable, like something from a museum.

"I'm going to miss my interview," she says, when Caitlin and I go out to visit. Her hair is braided into a horsetail, so long she has to rest it on one knee. Amazingly, the sun is hotter than before. Our socks have dried already on the railing, crisp as worms. "I'll have to be a baggage handler, like your father."

"He's a ramp agent," I say.

My mom just tightens her lips. Her face is glazed with sweat. I want to tell her something about my father. How he worked on Christmas morning last year, making triple time to pay for our presents. Or how I caught him once in the bathroom, smelling one of her old tennis shirts that he refused to wash.

"Did your father talk to you about living in Austin?"

Caitlin shakes her head.

"I should have known."

"We're moving?" Caitlin asks.

Mom looks at her lap. "It's up to you two. We both think it's a good idea. Your father needs some time, you know, to get his life together." She moves her braid from one knee to the other. "I'll be back in a couple weeks. You have time to think it over."

"Dad's not coming?" I ask.

My mother sighs. "Your dad—father—has a lot on his mind."

Caitlin looks at the porch. "How about if he gets his old job back?"

"Right. Ha. And I'll be singing with the Vienna Opera."

Mom says this in a voice I've never heard, curled in and disgusted. The kind you might use for smelly feet, or a food you can't stand. She fans herself with both hands.

"God, how can you stand this place!" She stands up and goes to the end of the porch, holding her tank top away from her back. When she lets go, it turns pink against her skin, like a magic trick. She turns around again, frowning. "I didn't mean that." She tries to smile and musses my hair. "Don't worry about Austin yet. Silent kid. How about one of your songs?"

I look at the street, at the moving water. I don't feel like making up any songs.

Later, Caitlin wakes me up in the middle of the night, whispering my name from the top bunk. She hangs her face off the edge, hair dandelioned from her head. She wants to know what the plan is. Outside the insects buzz and buzz, never rest. I tell her to go back to sleep, there aren't going to be any more plans.

"You said. If the other didn't work."

"It was all just pretend," I say. "Grow up."

"We stabbed the tires."

"*I* stabbed the tires! You didn't do anything."

She pulls her head from the edge. I can feel the volts of anger from her bunk. A car drives by on the street, slow as a bicycle, and you can see a movie of it on the wall.

"Mom came back," Caitlin says defiantly.

"She doesn't even look the same."

I get out of bed, pretending I have to pee. The carpet is limp and sweaty on my feet. My mother is sound asleep in the TV room, and I stop and watch her from the doorway. She's lying with her back to me, wearing a T-shirt that says BEAR SAFELY IN ALASKA. In the moonlight, I can make out the perfect twists of her braid. It hangs off the mattress, touching the floor. On the table beside her is the fake bone she brought from Alaska. Standing there by myself, I think of Zoomer, which makes me think of that dog in Japan, the one who waited at the station every day for his master's return. Imagine waiting all those years, picturing the ideal perfect ghost in your head.

The freezer light is on in the kitchen, glowing through the cracked-open door. Dad stuffed the box in as best he could. Maybe it will sit there after we're gone, a frozen secret, while my father grows old and gray and little.

Quietly, I peer into Dad's room on the other side of the kitchen. He's asleep like my mom, snoring with his mouth open. He looks peaceful under the covers, calm and smiling. I wonder if he's dreaming about Zoomer up in dog heaven. I close my eyes and have this vision of a place without people, cool as Alaska. Zoomer's there, of course, and the Mexican wolf, and the hummingbirds shooting around like sparks. The jaguarundi are just as famous as the jaguars. Oh give me a home, where the grizzly bears roam. Even the dermestid beetles are there, eating fruit and avoiding everyone's face. Everyone's happy. And in charge of it all is my father, Top Dog, earmuffs turned around his neck like a collar.

My dad stops snoring. I don't know how long I've been there. He sits up and switches on the lamp, blinking in the light.

"Don't cry," he says.

"I'm not."

"That's my job."

He scoots over, patting the space beside him. I crawl up in bed with him. He lets me under the sheet, where it's still warm from his body. A song starts to come to me, the first few words turning in my head.

There's some scampering in the hall. "Who's there?" Dad says.

Caitlin comes charging through the door. She's holding scissors. In the other hand, she lifts our mother's hair like a snake—grinning at me, ecstatic, waiting to be loved.

Mission

"OKAY, WHAT'S WRONG WITH THIS sentence?" Nils said, writing in large letters on the board because some of his students couldn't afford to buy glasses: BARKING LOUDLY IN CLASS, SVETLANA TOLD THE DOG TO BE QUIET OR IT MIGHT DISRUPT THE LESSON. He liked to use students as characters in his sentences, to help the class relate. Nils scanned the rows of squinting faces before glancing at the lump of pork buns sitting on his desk. Every day some new offering appeared there, native foods from China or El Salvador or Kazakhstan, home-cooked *blinis* or *pupusas*. Once, returning from a break at ten in the morning, he'd found a grease-stained paper bag filled with a bundled sheaf of chicken feet.

"What means 'disrupt'?" Noemi asked. Noemi had a proprietorial relationship with English and was angry when people used words she didn't know.

"Like 'interrupt,'" Nils explained. "To make the class stop."

"I no like this word," she said, shaking her head. "This word make me aggravate."

"Okay," Nils said patiently, erasing the word. "We'll change it to 'interrupt.' 'Barking loudly in class, Svetlana told the dog to be quiet or it might interrupt the lesson.' But what's wrong with this sentence?"

"I don't have a dog," Svetlana said in her meticulous Russian accent. It reminded Nils of someone trying to pick a safe with her teeth. Unlike most of the students at Arriba Language and Vocational School, she had impeccable grammar. "I don't understand this having dogs. They are very dirty creatures, and frequently lick you with the tongue. No one needs a dog licking you with the tongue, where other people kiss."

"Blind persons need dog," Noemi said.

"If I were blind, I would use a cane for dignity and not have a dirty creature take advantage of me."

"Not clean," Mei Ling said, nodding and holding her nose. She often ate dried fish in class and burped obstreperously, without apology. The Chinese women, who had to tackle a heroic language barrier, generally had the worst English in class. "In China, no dog come in house. Too much smell."

"Dogs very dirty," Zhao Jun agreed, bending to scribble something in her notebook. She carried the same notebook with her wherever she went. Once, when Nils was telling a joke to some students in the cafeteria during lunch, he'd seen her transcribing his words carefully, like a secretary taking minutes. Nils felt vaguely like he couldn't breathe.

"Okay, but imagine—for the sake of argument—that Svetlana has a dog. Hypothetically, right? What's wrong with this sentence?"

"You can't bring dogs to school!" Edwing said triumphantly from the back row. He worked at Safeway every night and spent most of class in a lizardlike trance.

"This is correct," Svetlana said, smiling at him. "Same with my little Yefim. I tried to bring him to school, but they wouldn't allow him in class for computers. No day care, so I ask you as full-time student, what can I do?"

"Put him to sleep," Edwing said equably.

"You don't understand." Svetlana turned white. "Yefim is not my dog."

"No should bring other person's dog to class," Mei Ling said. "Russians crazy."

"Crazy!" cried Zina, who always sat next to Svetlana. Since he'd started teaching at the school a month ago, Nils had rarely seen the two Russians part for more than a minute. Once, when Svetlana showed up to class with a new pair of sneakers, Zina had stared at them throughout the lesson and arrived the next day with an identical pair. "Eat foots of chicken, you call Russians crazy."

"Okay," Nils said weakly. He thought of the people in Dante's *Inferno,* rolling boulders in a half circle until they smashed into each other and had to retrace their steps. "Concentrate on the grammar, if you can. According to this sentence, who's doing the barking?"

"Dog's doing barking," Noemi said with supreme confidence.

"No," Nils said curtly. He turned to the corner of the classroom and looked at Lorena Poot, his last resort. Lorena was sixty years old and nearly toothless, a Latina woman with the sullen, breathtaking eyes of a Hollywood starlet. Though she didn't speak English perfectly, she studied harder than anyone in class and regularly scored 100 percent on the tests. "Please, Lorena—maybe you can tell the class. Who's doing the barking in this sentence?"

"Svetlana," she said indifferently, refusing to meet his eyes. "Modifier in the wrong place, like you talked about yesterday."

Nils thanked her with genuine gratitude, feeling the oxygen drain back into the room. He passed around a work sheet and put the students into pairs so they could wrestle with the answers together. The classroom was bare except for a sign on the back wall—SPELLING RULES—printed on a long flag of paper in faded, dot-matrix letters. Someone had taken down the actual rules, so that it seemed like an exuberant slogan devised by the board of education. Except for the drabness of the rooms—and despite days like this, when he feared his students weren't learning a thing—Nils loved teaching at the school. It was rowdy and unpredictable, gratifying in a way he couldn't explain. His parents, of course, thought he was crazy; if he was so bent on being a teacher, why not teach at a private school where he could earn a living? "What's this compulsion to save the world?"

Actually, Nils wasn't under any illusions about saving the world. From the outside, he knew there was something faintly ridiculous about a middle-class do-gooder teaching immigrants proper grammar. He thought of those tough-love teachers from Hollywood movies, inspiring gangbangers to find the area of a circle. But he had no desire to spoon-feed *The Great Gatsby* to a bunch of drowsy teenagers. He wanted to help people, however naïve that sounded: to teach people whose lives he could actually improve.

As usual, Lorena Poot refused to work with any of the other students, cutting a small and lonely figure in the corner, hunched over the handout like a prisoner hoarding a meal. Nils watched sadly as she scribbled out her answers. Her new dislike of him was baffling and seemed to exclude reason. Lately, when he was discussing some clear and indisputable law of grammar—the difference between "who" and "whom," say, or the past participle of "grow"—she would sigh disruptively and shake her head in disbelief, scoffing when he asked her what was wrong. The kinder Nils was, in fact, the more she seemed to hate him. As the class was leaving for the day, squaring their desks and rupturing into a Babel of languages, he called Lorena's name and asked her to stay behind for a few minutes.

"I want you to be happy in class," Nils said, sitting on the edge of his desk. He smiled and looked at the gold cross hanging flat against her sweater. Sometimes, between classes, he noticed Lorena sitting by herself in the corner of the cafeteria, her head bowed in prayer. "Tell me, please, is there something I did to make you angry?"

Lorena stared out the window. A lowrider floated by on the street, the Godzilla steps of a rap beat booming through the walls and rattling the chalkboard. "The last test," she said finally. For the first time, Nils noticed something peculiar about her nose—a gleaming smoothness out of keeping with the wrinkles of her face, like the burl of a log stripped of bark. "You put a question sign next to my sentence."

"That's right, sure," he said. "I remember you got one wrong. I didn't even count it because it was extra credit."

"My son is very smart, native speaker. He was raise here and speaks only English. He says there's nothing wrong with how I write."

"He's right, absolutely—you're an excellent writer." Nils walked to her desk, relieved. "If that's all it is, Lorena, I'm glad. Bring the sentence tomorrow, and we can talk about it."

"Tomorrow is Saturday, Mr. Rylander." He shrank slightly from her breath: a rottenish smell, like seaweed drying on the beach. Lorena reached into her bag and pulled out Nils's test, flipping to the extra credit section, where he'd asked them to write a sentence using a semicolon. She read her answer proudly, as if she were recording it for a tape. "I tried to cross the busy street with my son; however, the cars were an enemy."

"See there, Lorena. The grammar's fine." He put his hand

on her shoulder. "It's just we don't use the word 'enemy' quite like that."

"My son says you don't understand English."

"Your son?" he said, smiling.

"He thinks you're *poco inteligente*. Stupid."

Nils removed his hand from her shoulder. "Lorena," he said, clearing his throat. "I was born here. Even if I was stupid— which I don't think I am—I'd still be able to speak English."

"Born here!" Lorena looked him straight in the eye for the first time, her eyes damp and glowing. A look of radiant, unmistakable loathing. Nils was shocked to discover she was trembling. "So the rest of us, not born here, we don't deserve to be smarter than you!"

Nils didn't know what to say. He gathered himself to speak, but Lorena ducked behind her desk and grabbed the shopping bag she used to carry her books, stomping out of the classroom before he could defend himself.

After work, Nils walked to a protest rally he'd heard about from the other teachers at school. It was raining softly, a cobwebby tingle on his face. He headed in the same direction as his apartment, passing the little groceries and *panaderías* and "Mexicatessens," taking in the buoyant rush of Spanish that greeted him wherever he turned. Pot smoke drifted pleasantly from doorways. It was only five o'clock, but the Pentecostal church on Twenty-fourth Street was jammed with people; Nils stopped for a second and peered in at the service, listening to the heartfelt sputter of tambourines. He liked to walk around the neighborhood at this time of day because there were so many people outside, milling about on the sidewalk, playing baseball or barbecuing steaks by the curb or scratching at a lottery card with a toddler cleaving to one hip. The Mission District—at least the part he lived in—made the world of college seem bland and lethargic. Originally, he'd moved here after graduating with the expectation of befriending his neighbors. He'd imagined borrowing Nicaraguan spices, trading his jazz CDs for broken-hearted *ranchera* music. His first day in the apartment, he'd left the door open to greet well-wishers. No one had come. Even now, his neighbors seemed to ignore him on purpose, averting their eyes as he passed them on the sidewalk.

Nearing Bryant Street, he paused in front of a small playground to watch two boys horsing around on the swing set. One was standing on the swing, gripping the chains and swinging in jagged parabolas over the second one, who lay on his back among the orange peels and condoms littering the concrete. The metal seat of the swing brushed over the supine boy's face, which made him shriek with terror and giggle deliriously. For a second, watching them play, Nils felt a fragile sort of weepiness he'd come to associate with living in the city. He thought of Lorena Poot: aside from some petty grudges in high school, he'd never had someone hate him before.

He walked up to Mission Street, alert to the expanding number of cafés and trendy-looking thrift stores. The rally was being sponsored by the Anti-Displacement Coalition. The protesters—about twenty-five or thirty of them—were gathered around the construction site of a newly begun office development, undeterred by the increasing drizzle. People in raincoats or hooded capes blocked the sidewalk and carried homemade signs, mounted placards that read EVICTION KILLS CULTURE or THANKS, MAYOR BROWN, FOR HELPING US OUT. Nils stood on the corner and watched them protest, impressed by the diversity of the crowd. Except for Nils, most of the white people there had face piercings and Puma tennis shoes. There was a banner tied to the fence of the construction site, a giant, silk-screened picture of a scared-looking Latino man crouched in an alley and wearing a sombrero. Above the picture was the mock headline LAST REMAINING MEXICAN FOUND IN MISSION DISTRICT.

While Nils wiped the rain from his face, an actual man in a sombrero stood next to the banner and made a fiery speech about keeping the Mission home to immigrants and artists. Nils guessed the sombrero was an ironic gesture. When he'd finished his speech, the man led the protesters in a chant, clapping out "We're not on loan, so yuppies go home!" until the whole throng had taken up his words. The protesters shook their signs as they yelled, inciting passersby to join the chant. Nils chanted as well, caught up in the protesters' fury. He was impressed by the volume of their anger, but what struck him more than anything was the illusion of a single shout: all the gleaming, different-colored faces, chanting in a perfect euphony of voices.

That night, Nils decided to throw a party for his students. He made up an invitation on a piece of construction paper and drew a map to his address, tracing a long arrow from the school and wending it through the eight blocks of urban streets to the door of his apartment. The arrow thrilled him, for some reason. At the top of the invitation, he wrote POTLUCK AT NILS'S: BRING YOUR FAVORITE DISH. It was against school policy, probably, but Nils wanted to bridge the authoritarian divide between himself and his students.

Mostly, though, Nils thought it would be fun. When he handed the invitations out on Monday, Noemi squinted at her copy and asked, "Who is this Nils?"

"Me," he explained. "That's my name."

"You, teacher?" Mei Ling said. She looked at him skeptically, her eyes drifting down his body. "You need dishes?"

"No, I don't need dishes. 'Dish' means 'food' sometimes. It's a party. Cook your favorite food and bring it over for everyone to try." He looked at Edwing in the back. "What's your favorite food, Edwing?"

Edwing thought for a minute. "McDonald's."

"I see. Do you have any other favorite foods?"

"Shrimps. I like them a lot."

"Oh," Nils said encouragingly, "what kind of shrimp?"

"You know, the type you get from Sizzler."

"Right. I was hoping you guys would bring dishes from your own countries. Traditional un-Sizzler food? *Pupusas* maybe? Like the food you put on my desk."

The class looked at Svetlana, as they often did when they didn't understand something completely. She touched her hair and stood up, facing them from the front row. "We should cook homemade food and bring it in Tupperware," she explained. "Everyone shall eat at our teacher's house, to taste the lost nourishment of our countries."

Of course, Nils couldn't have said it so beautifully, with the same Russian contempt for banality. The class broke into a bedlam of voices, inspecting the invitations and glancing at the street sign through the window to check the map's veracity. Nils felt a deep flush of pleasure. He'd developed a great affection for his students; just last week, he'd sat with Svetlana and several other students after class, talking about the global spread of American culture and leafing through elaborately staged pictures of their families. At the rear of the classroom, Lorena Poot seemed barely in control of her face, lips clamped together but moving strangely at the same time, as if she were shelling a sunflower seed with her tongue. She had folded the invitation into a small square and placed it at the very top of her desk, like a dirty Kleenex. Weirdly, Nils found himself craving her approval. Her eyes were clear and beautiful, and for a moment he forgot himself, mesmerized by the ferocity of her stare.

"You always itch!" she said in a strange voice.

"What?"

"None of the other teachers itch!" She was almost shouting. "I don't understand it. But you! Itch and itch and itch!"

The class had gone silent, leaning in their chairs to look at Lorena.

"What do you mean?" Nils asked, bewildered.

"You itch like a *mono*. Monkey!"

"Scratch? You're angry at me because I scratch, Lorena?"

"You itch your head, everywhere. Always itching." She scratched her head and chest in pantomime, like a mad woman beset by fleas. Mei Ling started to giggle. "None of the other teachers itch in class, so it makes me wonder why you're hired."

"Lorena, I don't know what you mean," Nils said quietly. He took a step backward and bumped into his desk, trying to keep his voice steady. "If you have a problem, calm down and speak to me after class."

He walked to the blackboard and began to outline the three planning criteria for an interoffice memo. PURPOSE . . . AUDIENCE . . . MAIN IDEA. When he was done, he turned to see Lorena mocking him behind his back, hunched over her desk and scratching her head and armpit in a crazed allergic spasm. Her lips were peeled back to look like a monkey's. Some of the students were laughing, and Nils tried to see it as an attempt at humor. Except it wasn't funny—it was nightmarish and grotesque, this toothless woman scratching herself without mercy. He did his best to ignore her. Finally—after the third or fourth time—he swung around suddenly and slammed the textbook he was holding down on his desk.

"Lorena, stop it! You're disrupting the class, like a five-year-old! I have to ask you to leave."

"My son never itches," she said, standing from her desk with a look of triumph. "He's your age and has perfect manners."

Nils looked away from her, his heart leaping once to calm

itself. "Leave the class until you can settle down and act respect-fully."

Lorena grabbed her shopping bag of belongings and swung it at no one in particular, muttering in Spanish as she stomped across the room. She looked wild, her hair puffed into a cloud cap. She turned and spat in Nils's direction, a thread of saliva sticking to her chin, before slamming the door behind her. Her footsteps banged down the hall. She was mentally ill, no doubt about it. The only alternative, which Nils refused to accept, was that she despised him so much it drove her beyond reason.

"Lady go look for her marbles," Noemi said, orbiting an ear with her finger, and he had to keep himself from siding openly with the class.

After the other teachers had left, Nils stayed at the school and helped the education coordinator with busywork, making flyers and hunting down the janitor so they could fix a leak in the computer room. He tried to keep his mind on what he was doing, but the image of Lorena Poot's trembling face disrupted his thoughts, flashing in his head like a jammed or broken slide. He pictured her wandering the neighborhood, scratching her armpits at strangers. On his way to the teachers' room, he stopped in the student services office to see if he could look at Lorena's file.

"No history of mental illness," said the student services manager, a former student who threatened to quit before the beginning of each month but always showed up on the first with a sheepish look of contempt. "One of the walk-ins. Not on meds, far as we know."

"Do you know anything about her life?"

"*Es muy trágica.* Her husband's in jail for battery. All the time used to beat her and her kid." She leaned over her desk. "*Fíjate.* I'm not supposed to tell you, but I know this from the case manager's file. This husband bit off her nose."

"What?"

"That's what it says, if you can believe. Went berserk and bit her nose off—most of it, anyway. They had to . . . what do you call? *Reconstruir.* Build again from scratch."

At home that night, Nils glanced out the window and saw two people standing on the far side of the street, half hidden by a withered sapling, staring up at his dark apartment through the glare of an arc lamp. It was Lorena Poot, peering through the branches like a ghostly incarnation of his thoughts. She was clutching something in her hand, a white paper she'd rolled into a wand. Nils wondered if it was the invitation he'd handed out in class. Beside her was a young man twice her size, his long face caved into a scowl, dressed unseasonably in a scarf and corduroy blazer. He looked like a hit man dressed up for a picnic. The man reached up and scratched his head. Breathless, Nils opened the window and said Lorena's name. She stepped back, startled by his voice. "Wait!" Nils cried. She turned and began to walk off, yanking at the sleeve of her accomplice, who gave Nils a fearless and vindictive look before heeding his mother's tugs. Nils wanted to tell her something important, maybe even indispensable, but he couldn't think what it was. He went downstairs and unlatched the front door and ran out in his socks, calling to them from his gated stoop, but they had already left.

The next day in class, glancing at the empty desk in the corner, Nils felt a strange and unnavigable sorrow; there was a splotch of yellow paint on the chair, as if Lorena Poot had melted in her seat and left a buttery stain in her place. Sometimes, straying to her side of the room, he thought he could smell the toothless odor of her breath. He should have been relieved, considering how well the class got on without her; but this new, easy rapport made Nils feel ashamed. Watching students work together on a run-on sentence exercise, he felt adrift from his own legs as he wove the aisles. He mentioned Lorena Poot's name to the other teachers, who seemed unconcerned, even blasé. Students dropped out all the time—it was just the nature of the demographic they served. Though he knew it was wishful thinking, Nils held out a secret hope that Lorena would show up for his party.

On Friday night, Nils lost himself in the rush of getting ready. He hung a sign on the front gate that said WORLD FEAST IN APT. B, watching for guests and feeling a twirl of hidden pride that his neighbors would see people with faces similar to their own arriving at his door. He knew the pride was wrong, perhaps even racist—but he couldn't help it. He wondered if he'd invited Jack and Melissa, schoolmates from college who lived in town, simply to show off his students. No, they were his friends: it would be worse *not* to invite them, to segregate your friendships according to class.

"*Híjole*. Too much space for live alone," said Noemi, who arrived twenty minutes early with a giant stockpot and a bag full of groceries. Noemi's bangs were sprayed into delicate strands belling crisply from her scalp, like a row of question marks floating over her eyes. She went directly into the kitchen and pulled a white apron from her bag. Amazed, Nils watched her tie the apron around her waist and start cooking something on the stove, chopping onions and cilantro on the bare linoleum of his counter.

"Noemi, please," he said. "You don't have to cook. It's a party."

"Oh no, very easy. *Caldo de pollo*. You will eat like orphan."

He had an uneasy feeling that she'd misconstrued the point of the party. Nils felt better when the Chinese students arrived, bearing giant boxes of store-bought dim sum and filling the kitchen with a gummy, nectarous smell. They were dressed in high heels and windbreakers, like a varsity squad of ballroom dancers. After unboxing each dish and mounding them onto plates, the women inspected Nils's kitchen with deep and silent interest, seeming especially fascinated by his refrigerator, whose door was plastered with photographs. One photo, taken at a New Year's Eve party in college and showing Nils kissing a casual acquaintance amorously on the lips, drew the most attention. Mei Ling said something in Cantonese, and the women all burst into laughter. They talked comically for a minute and then Mei Ling grew serious, her lips drawn into a scowl.

She asked Nils why he put pictures up on the refrigerator for everyone to see.

"I don't know," Nils said, taken aback by her vehemence. Did he want people to know he had friends? "Just a custom, I guess."

Mei Ling glanced toward the stove and leaned into a whisper. "But your housekeeper—she can look at private life? She can stare at your secret kissing?"

Nils's heart sank. "That's not my housekeeper. It's Noemi. Noemi Lopez, from class."

"She works very hard," Zhao Jun said, equally serious. "Cook each and every night."

"No, listen. She's a guest like you! You know her from class. Noemi, turn around and show them."

Noemi turned from the stove with a haggard expression. The question marks of her bangs had steamed into squiggles, pasted flat across her forehead. "Cook and clean, like slave— he is more bad than my husband."

The doorbell rang and Nils went to answer it, hearing a bright burst of laughter as he left the kitchen, realizing only then—Noemi's voice repeating his words in broken English—that they'd played a joke on him. He felt relieved and vexed at the same time. Before long the apartment was jammed with people. Zina and Svetlana arrived wearing the same blue eye shadow, bearing Tupperware containers filled with *pelmeni* and a remarkable salad that looked like a stratified cross section of the Grand Canyon. "Herring in a Fur Coat," Svetlana called it. Not surprisingly, Jack and Melissa were the last ones to show up, squeezing through the crowd with a plate of steamed artichokes and a ceramic bowl of mayonnaise. There were so many entrées that Nils moved some of them to the living room, setting up a card table and stacking it with paper plates, the dark pane of the window smudging with steam. Guests helped themselves to dinner, shuttling between portions of *pelmeni* and *caldo de pollo,* though Nils couldn't help noticing that people stayed pretty faithful to their own contributions. The "Herring in a Fur Coat" was studiously avoided by the Chinese students, just as Zina and Svetlana avoided the doughy balls of dim sum glistening like jellyfish. Jack and Melissa made a concerted effort to interest guests in the artichokes, showing a cadre of Chinese women how to scrape a leaf clean with their teeth. Jack offered some artichoke to Zhao Jun, who nibbled gallantly at one end and then stuffed the remaining leaf in her coat pocket. "Very good," she said, smiling. "I keep to show husband."

Nils alone tried to sample all the cuisines, heaping everything on one plate and encouraging the promiscuous blending of sauces. There was no more space on the floor of the living room, and he ate standing up. Remembering how Melissa had spent a college semester in Guatemala, he coaxed her from the card table and introduced her to a group of Latina students passing photographs on the couch. She told them a story about getting strip-searched in Flores, recounting the anecdote in slang-filled Spanish; the students seemed far more interested in her pierced lip than in her travels. Melissa showed them her tongue as well, a single stud nesting there like a pearl, which caused Amada Espinoza to cross herself with her eyes closed. Surveying the room, Nils was dismayed by how quickly his guests had broken into groups, dividing themselves by race and culinary preference, but he counted on people mingling after their meal was done and tried not to worry about it.

But even after dinner Nils's guests remained ensconced in their groups, speaking Cantonese or Russian or Spanish in schoolyardish cliques. The Chinese women cleaned their teeth in the corner, shielding their mouths demurely with one hand. Even Jack and Melissa gave up socializing eventually, discussing last week's episode of *Sex and the City* at one end of the couch. After a while, out of frustration, Nils moved to the center of the room and announced that they'd play a game together as a group.

"What kind of game?" Zina asked.

"Charades," he said, because it was the only game he could think of. Jack groaned. "We'll take turns acting out the names of different things. One team acts out the name without talking, and everyone has to guess what it is. Like a secret." The room was silent. "Okay. Right. I'll go first, to demonstrate."

Partly to punish him, Nils grabbed Jack and pulled him to the center of the room. He decided to do a movie, trying to think of a film famous enough that everyone would know about it. He whispered the name in Jack's ear and then started acting out the first word of the title, tracing a star in the air with his finger. Jack followed his lead, making a halfhearted attempt to accompany his mimes. When the star failed to elicit a response, Nils looked up and pointed at the sky, gesturing with two hands, which caused many of the guests to stare at the ceiling and murmur to each other. It occurred to him that his guests believed they were watching a play. With a growing sense of doom, Nils moved on to the second word and lowered himself to a soldier's crouch, skulking around the floor and pretending to shoot Jack, who stared at him with an authentically savage regard for the enemy. After a few minutes, feeling desperate, Nils stopped in front of Melissa and pleaded with his eyes for help. Some of the Chinese women started to clap.

"*Reservoir Dogs?*" Melissa said.

"Right!" Nils said. He stole a look at Jack, who smirked. "I mean no. Close. It was *Star Wars.*"

"I thought star," Svetlana said, nodding. "But why do the stars commit war?"

"It's a movie," Nils said. It occurred to him *Star Wars* probably had a different name in their country. "Luke Skywalker? Darth Vader?" He looked around the room, suddenly exasperated. He tried to think of an enduring figure from the film, someone mythic enough to transcend cultures. "You've never heard of Chewbacca?"

"R2-D2," Edwing said, the first words he'd spoken all night. He was sitting by himself on Nils's stereo speaker.

"R2-D2, yes!"

"His friend is C-3PO."

Nils was overjoyed. "C-3PO!" he said to the Chinese women, who smiled and continued cleaning their teeth. Zhao Jun opened her notebook and wrote something down. He felt encouraged. "Okay, your turn. Mei Ling, everybody? Choose your topic."

"We don't know which topic," Mei Ling said.

"Anything. A song maybe. Go up and act out the name of a song."

The Chinese women looked at each other and then stood up reluctantly, drifting to the middle of the room with solemn expressions. Mei Ling said something to the group, and they began to speak heatedly in Cantonese, arguing—Nils suspected—over what to perform.

Lai Chu, a Mandarin-speaking woman with a perpetual cold, seemed bewildered by the proceedings. While the other women conferred, she wandered to the card table where the entrées were set up and studied the food through her glasses. Before Nils could warn her, she plucked one of the artichoke leaves and popped the whole thing in her mouth. Nils watched her chew the leaf with stoic resolve, not wanting to embarrass her in front of the party. He looked ruefully at his watch, ready to give up on the game altogether. As the Chinese students argued, Lai Chu drifted toward the group and then stepped through the tumult of voices, commanding the room's attention. Inspired, she started to pace back and forth in a vigorous mime, flapping her arms up and down. The Chinese women regarded her with amazement and then flapped their arms as well, a roomful of panicked birds.

"'The Flight of the Bumblebee,'" Melissa said.

Noemi jumped up. "Chickens in war!"

Lai Chu stopped flapping and pointed at her mouth. She pretended to gasp, turning a deep crimson and clutching the arm of the couch.

"'Every Breath You Take,'" Zina said. "By Police band. This famous song in Russia."

"I think she's choking," Jack said.

Nils leaped up to save her, but Edwing had already jumped off the speaker and grabbed Lai Chu by the waist, smacking her on the back with the base of his fist. The artichoke leaf flew from her mouth and struck the window. Lai Chu dropped to her knees on the floor, breathing in deep, sputtering gasps, her glasses dangling from one ear. Nils's guests crowded around her to make sure she was all right. Catching her breath finally, Lai Chu tottered to her feet and tamped down her hair, face glowing with vanquished terror, as if she'd just dived successfully from a cliff. Nils wondered if he should call an ambulance, but she seemed to have recovered. Tenderly, with a mother's instinct, Zina unhooked Lai Chu's glasses and fixed them again to her face. Nobody touched the errant artichoke leaf, which had snailed down the window in a half-chewed pulp.

For the next half hour Edwing held the attention of the crowd, goaded into recounting his rescue while Nils's students interrupted here and there to make him more heroic, swarming him with toasts. Edwing blushed at their praise but didn't refute it. Beneath his pleasure and relief, Nils felt a faint tinge of jealousy. He couldn't help reflecting that, despite his best efforts as host, only an aborted tragedy seemed to bring everyone together.

Predictably, Jack and Melissa were the first to leave, explaining that they had a "circus rave" to go to in Oakland. The rave was supposed to have fire dancers and an actual live tiger. Seeing them out the door, Nils was surprised by how glad he felt to be left alone with his students.

"The Chinese women are adorable," Melissa said, kissing his cheek on the front stoop.

Turning back to his apartment, Nils noticed a sheet of paper posted like an advertisement to his door. A page of *e* words photocopied from a dictionary. At the top of the page, someone had scrawled in big letters YOU SHOULD LEARN ENGLISH BEFORE DECIDING TO BE TEACHER! The note was signed "Fausto Poot (son of Lorena)." About halfway down the page, the same person had circled part of an entry in red ink:

> enemy \ `en e me, -mi\ *n, pl* enemies [< L *in-*, not + *amicus,* friend] 1: one that seeks the injury, overthrow, or failure of a person or thing to which he is opposed: ADVERSARY, OPPONENT 2: something injurious, harmful, or deadly (drink was his greatest ~)

The second definition was highlighted in yellow marker. A soggy despair seeped into Nils's bones. He pulled the paper from his door, detaching each of the corners with care and folding it into his pocket. He went back inside and started to clean up the kitchen, which was an incredible mess. Guests strolled in and out, sobering their faces for Nils's benefit and asking if they could help. After a while he told people to go home, and they obeyed him as if he were a teacher, stacking their plates and Tupperware with complaisant smiles and shuffling out the door.

Later that night, Nils woke from a dream, his heart clocking in his throat. He couldn't stop imagining Lorena Poot's face in the dark. He got up finally and went to the living room and finished the cleaning he'd started before bed. Straightening the couch, he found a photograph stuck between two cushions, a Polaroid of Noemi and two people who looked to be her sisters. She had her arms looped around their shoulders, smiling extravagantly at the camera, standing in the busy square of a Latin American city. The background was blurred, but you could see the scaffold of a market stall with a row of leather bags hanging from a rope. On the back of the picture, someone had written: *Navidad 1998. Te extrañamos mucho.* We miss you very much. Nils was overwhelmed. He had no idea, actually, what his students had left behind. He stared at the photograph for a long time and then hung it on the refrigerator in the kitchen, covering up the foolish image of him kissing.

Surprisingly, at least compared to his own predictions, Nils's students made progress in the class. By the end of spring, most of them could write a simple office memo that was—if not free of errors—at least comprehensible to a native speaker. And there were other successes as well, both in and out of the classroom. Edwing, who'd gained greatly in popularity since saving Lai Chu's life, seemed like a different person in class, calling out answers from the back of the room and joking with the Chinese women as if they were old friends. Once, walking to the bathroom during lunch break, Nils was astonished to see Edwing and Lai Chu posed erotically in an empty classroom, the shy and pleasant Safeway worker stripped half naked on the teacher's desk. A grid of glass bulbs suctioned Edwing's body; Lai Chu knelt beside him, guarding some empty bulbs by her knees and surveying the mottled field of his back. She lit a match under one of the empty bulbs and then cupped it quickly to a space near Edwing's hip, so that a pinkish swell of skin plumped into the bulb and filled it with an Edwingy glow.

"I am almost cupped," Edwing said, smiling at Nils when he entered the room. "Lai Chu is an expert in China. You should try for your stress."

And one day Svetlana came to class with her hair pinned in a stylish chignon, wearing gold earrings and an expensive-looking skirt. She announced that she'd gotten a job at an insurance office and was set to start tomorrow. When Mei Ling asked her how much it paid, Svetlana blushed proudly and refused to answer.

"Sixteen dollars an hour," Zina said, beaming at her friend's good fortune.

It was more than Nils made. It dawned on him, shamefully, that he hadn't truly expected any of them to get jobs.

"That's fantastic," he said, moved. "Svetlana, really. That's amazing news. You'll be managing the place in no time."

On his way home, though, Nils felt an unlikely gust of sadness. He decided to stop by another protest for the Anti-Displacement Coalition, heading down Twenty-first Street instead of his usual route. A small yet bustling *carnicería*—one that Nils used to shun because of the smell, actually crossing the street to avoid feeling ill—had disappeared without a trace, transformed into a Bikram yoga center with a rainbow painted over the door. Nils wondered if he had the wrong address until he looked down and saw a faint stain of blood on the sidewalk. The protest was being held in front of a multimedia office center that, before its fancy new conversion, had housed some small businesses and nonprofit agencies. Protesters crowded the doors, shouting anticorporate slogans and spilling into the street. Nils recognized many of their signs from last time; it disheartened him somehow that they hadn't bothered to make new ones. There was a lectern set up on the sidewalk, and the same man as before—the charismatic Latino with the sombrero—mounted the podium and started to talk about corporate-sponsored fascism, how the "Goliath of big business" was waging a war on the underclass. The crowd cheered at the end of each sentence, hissing unanimously whenever the man said the word "yuppie." It all seemed true of course, just as before, but for some reason the hyperbole depressed Nils. It seemed flashy and naïve, disproportionate to the number of protesters. If it were truly a Goliath—this heartless corporate world that included insurance companies—then what chance, really, did they stand against it?

Scanning the crowd, Nils recognized Lorena Poot standing a short distance from the lectern, watching the protest with the young man he'd caught spying on his apartment the night before his party. The man was wearing the same scarf and corduroy jacket, even in the sunny warmth of May. He seemed distracted, glancing around indifferently and fidgeting with his scarf. Worried he'd lose them again, Nils waved across the crowd until Lorena's son noticed him from afar. The young man lurched forward without warning and headed straight for Nils, bumping through the knot of protesters, a look of calm yet purposeful belligerence on his face. It looked like he meant to knife Nils in the stomach. Nils clenched his fists, trying to remember the two or three jujitsu moves he'd learned as a teenager. The man stopped in front of him and stared at Nils without speaking.

"Do you like Pokémon candy?" he demanded finally. His breath smelled like peanut butter.

"No," Nils stammered. "I mean, I don't know. I've never tried it."

"I like Pokémon candy," he said in a confidential way. "It tastes like fruity flavors."

The man's face had a sleepy sort of strangeness, like a boxer's after a fight, and a yellow glob of snot clotted his nostril. Nils's muscles unfroze, a gentle thawing in his veins. "Are you Fausto Poot?" Nils asked. "That's your mother?"

"My mother doesn't like Bulbasaur. She doesn't even like Pikachu."

Nils glanced up and saw Lorena observing them from the verge of protesters, her face a deep and startling red. She ducked through the protesters until Nils had lost her in the crowd. He wanted to race after her but couldn't just leave her son, who was ogling a butch woman in a sleeveless T-shirt, staring at the tattoo of a black widow crawling up her neck. Standing on his toes, Nils thought he saw Lorena's small figure reappear down the sidewalk, crossing Mission Street without looking and then vanishing behind the busy corner of Twenty-fifth.

"Fausto," Nils said, addressing him sternly. "Where do you live?"

"San Francisco, California."

"Okay," he said, nodding. "Me, too. And what street do you live on?"

Fausto regarded him with sudden contempt. "I'm not supposed to tell."

"Right. Of course." Nils looked at his watch, wondering what to do. He tried, unsuccessfully, to imagine a humiliation so severe that you'd abandon your own son. Fausto seemed to take an interest in Nils's watch as well, staring at the digital face as if it were a rare and expensive coin.

"How much does your watch cost?" he asked.

"I don't remember. Not very much."

Fausto pushed up the sleeve of his coat, showing him the imitation Rolex squeezing his wrist. The face was crosshatched with scratches. Fausto loosened the watchband and slid it off his wrist, which was marked with a Lilliputian tractor tread. It took Nils a minute to realize he wanted to trade.

"Okay, tell you what," Nils said, inspired. "I'll trade with you—for an hour—but you have to take me to your house. Your mother's already gone home. You wear my watch and I'll wear yours. You don't have to tell me anything . . . just show me where you live."

Fausto strapped Nils's dime-store Casio to his wrist, dropping to one knee on the sidewalk to steady himself. Nils knelt as well and helped him buckle the plastic strap. Fausto didn't seem at all worried about his mother's disappearance. Rising cautiously, he threaded his way through the crowd and then broke into a brisk and imperious march, keeping his head down as he walked. Nils had to rush to keep up with him. They turned up Twenty-fifth Street and walked for a long time before veering down Florida, heading in the direction of Cesar Chavez, reaching a trash-strewn block lined with runtish trees and bland, stucco-walled apartment houses. Curtains were drawn in all the windows. There were old cars parked on the sidewalk, some of them stranded with flats or smashed up like Coke cans, so that Fausto and Nils had to weave around them and edge into the street. A dog paced one of the roofs, barking furiously at them from above. Fausto looked up and barked back.

Abruptly, he crossed the street and stopped in front of a fifties-style apartment house with filthy windows, pausing at the garage door next to the steps. The paint on the garage door was chipped and flaking into scales.

Nils realized, his uneasiness cresting into fear, that the man was lost.

"Fausto!" he said sharply. "That's somebody's garage."

Ignoring him, Fausto gripped the rusty handle, slid the door halfway up its tracks, and ducked inside. Nils crossed the street after him, wondering how he'd explain to the police what he was about to do. He crouched down but couldn't get low enough to see anything. Hesitantly, he followed Fausto under the garage door and stood up into a large, well-kept space, surprised to find that the lights were on. An antique pickup with blue California plates stood in the middle of the garage, scorched by a fringe of rust. Nils's eyes adjusted to the light and he started to notice other details as well: a Formica table jutting from behind the pickup and set carefully with silverware, a twin bed in the nearest corner made to immaculate perfection, a muddle of pots covering one wall and dangling over a Coleman stove attached to a propane tank. Near the bed was a large gray refrigerator, its doors flung open to reveal a row of shirts hanging from a wire. The shirts were creased down the sleeves and beautifully ironed.

Slowly, Nils walked around the pickup until he could see a smaller room in the back of the garage, the walls narrowing into a sort of alcove, carpeted and fully furnished. Lorena Poot sat in a couch against the wall. Her face was flushed, the controls of a Nintendo console scattered near her feet. Nils stopped beside the front wheel of the pickup, half hidden by the ridge of the fender. Despite the disconcerting presence of the truck, he was impressed by the largeness of the garage, how much bigger it was than his own apartment. On the TV across from Lorena was a vase of fresh-cut lilies.

She asked Fausto, who was sitting on the rug and untying his shoes with two hands, where he'd been.

"The man gave me a watch," he blurted, showing her the Casio. He glanced back in Nils's direction. Something—the fragile intimacy of the scene, perhaps—prevented Nils from revealing himself right away. Lorena blanched and stood up from the couch, unaware of his hiding place behind the pickup.

"Take it off right now," she said angrily. *"Ese hombre no es tu padre."*

She grabbed Fausto's wrist and clawed the watchband with her fingers, trying to undo the buckle with one hand. He leaped to his feet and pulled his arm from her grasp. For a second, before realizing Fausto was on the verge of tears, Nils thought the man might strike his mother.

"It's time for your bath," Lorena said, turning away. She kept her eyes down, as if ashamed of her outburst. "You smell like a *ranchero*. Take off the watch or you will ruin it."

Fausto wiped his eyes with the sleeve of his jacket, a bubble of snot blooming from one nostril. In the excitement, he seemed to have forgotten about Nils—or perhaps accepted that he'd gone home. Lorena walked over to an old claw-foot tub on the far side of the garage, turning a brace of spigots on the wall and adjusting the squeaky knobs for temperature. The tub was right out in the open, next to a folding screen that formed a private room in the corner, concealing what Nils guessed to be a toilet. A sculpture of Jesus on the cross hung conspicuously above the tub.

Nils was about to emerge from his hiding place—to face Lorena's wrath and guiltily return the watch, maybe even work up the courage to ask her back to school—when Fausto began taking his clothes off, struggling out of his shirt and pants until he was stark naked in the middle of the garage. His body, freed of clothes, was strong and hairless and magnificent. He looked athletic, even graceful. Barefoot, he padded over to the tub against the wall, beelining halfway across the floor before pausing deliberately to scratch his head—a nervous tic Nils had seen earlier but only now discerned as habit.

As the tub filled, rattling a pipe against the wall, Nils noticed a framed picture hung above the stove in the kitchen. The picture showed Fausto and Lorena standing on some steps, posing with a grinning man who looked to be in his sixties; though he couldn't be sure, Nils thought he recognized the strip of silver glinting from the man's wrist as the watch he was wearing.

He knew that he should leave, that he was snooping on Lorena's poverty, but he felt a secret, adversarial thrill at living up to her opinion of him.

Fausto got into the tub, and Lorena knelt beside him on the concrete floor, tucking the gold cross she wore into her sweater. She dunked her son in the water and started cleaning him carefully with a sponge. She soaped each limb with long, worshipful strokes, singing a child's melody in Spanish, lifting his arms gently to reach the pale of his armpits. Her voice, like her eyes, was beautiful and startling. When she got to his feet, she sponged each toe with particular care, taking time to scrub under the nails. The movement of the water made flamelike squiggles on the ceiling. Lorena paused to wipe the steam from her face, beginning a different song. For some reason, the irrational beauty of it made Nils angry. When she'd finished, Lorena remained on her knees and pressed the sponge against the nape of her neck, as if to relieve a pain.

"Is it prayer time?" Fausto asked.

"Yes," she said. "I'm glad you remind me. Who today should we pray for?"

Fausto laughed, splashing the water with his feet. "Maybe the man with bad English."

Lorena stiffened. She dropped the hand from her neck. "Mr. Rylander?"

"He likes Pokémon candy, I think."

She turned to look at Fausto, sharply, just enough for Nils to see the dark contortion of her face. Her son seemed to have lost interest in the topic, sliding deeper into the tub until he was submerged to the chin. Water dripped from the spigots and *pleek*ed into the tub. After a minute, Lorena nodded at no one in particular and glanced at the Jesus dying on the wall. She reached under her sweater and pulled out the cross. Then she clasped her hands and rested her forehead against the rim of the tub. Her hair had come down in front, slipping from its bun so that the loose strands coiled in the water. She started to murmur something in Spanish, her voice low and reverent. Nils couldn't understand a word. She mentioned his name, Señor Rylander, and Fausto looked up from the tub. He seemed to be staring in Nils's direction. A breeze swept under the garage door and lifted the hairs on Nils's neck. When Lorena finished her prayer, Fausto broke his gaze and glanced back at his knees. He said "Amen," pronouncing it like his mother's Spanish.

Nils rose from his crouch and crept out of the garage as silently as he could.

Rather than the exception, Svetlana turned out to be the rule: several of Nils's students got placed in jobs even before they graduated, making considerably more money than they'd expected. Nils was surprised at first, watching them leave school suddenly and head out for jobs at Mexicana Airlines or Crane Pest Control, their foreheads breaking out from excitement. The students credited Nils for their success, showering him with exotic gifts. Strangely, though, walking home with a set of Russian nesting dolls or a year's supply of ginseng tea,

Nils had a vague sense of having betrayed them. As the cycle wound down, and more and more students got jobs, he found himself staring out the window during assignments, or checking the clock to see how much time remained in class. Whereas before he'd walked around the room and helped slower students with their exercises, tutoring them in verbals or subordinating clauses, now he sat at his desk and waited passively for them to finish. Obviously, he was thrilled they were finding jobs—so why was he depressed? He wondered if he'd hoped for more than that, but what the "more" was he couldn't say. He told himself that his students were entering the economic mainstream, that they were tangibly better off than before they came to school, but it didn't erase the fact that they were leaving him.

The final week of classes, on Monday, Nils was rushing from the copy room on his way to job preparation class when he saw Lorena Poot in the reception area. She was sitting with a shopping bag in her lap, her knees tucked primly together. He had to fight the urge to duck down the hall. Lorena stood up when she saw him but refused to meet his eyes.

"Lorena?" Nils said, catching his breath. "How long have you been here?"

"You have my son's watch." She dug in the shopping bag and pulled out Nils's Casio.

"Yes, I'm sorry. I was going to get your phone number, from student services, but haven't had time." The truth was, he'd been avoiding calling her. "Look, it's at home on my desk. The watch. I have class right now." He stopped and took a deep breath. A BB of sweat rolled from his armpit. Nils glanced at the recruitment flyers taped to the inside of the front door, remembering the excitement he used to feel walking through it every morning. He forced himself to lie. "I hoped, when I saw you, that maybe you wanted to come back to school."

Lorena stared at the Casio without responding. The watch, fogged to an unreadable mist, trembled from her fingers. "I didn't come to hear you teach," she said defiantly, dropping her hand.

"You don't have to. Not today, anyway. The students are doing presentations." He watched her fumble with her bag. "What about sitting in class? For an hour? I was going to go home for lunch anyway—I can get the watch then."

"You don't teach?"

"They're talking about themselves, to practice their speaking. About an interesting event from their past."

Lorena looked up from her bag. Her eyes scoured his face, as though she were seeing him for the first time. Nils wondered if he looked different than she remembered.

"Why do you need so much that we talk like you?"

"It's not me, Lorena." He gestured, alluding to the world outside.

"You seem like a very lonely man, Mr. Rylander. Perhaps you itch out of loneliness. Crazy itcher. I am like an itch, so you ask me to sit in your class and learn to talk." She lowered her voice, which remained oddly calm despite the intensity of her eyes. "In this case, only for today, I will help you."

Nils stared at her, at a loss for words. He excused himself for class and then went to the men's room and stood by the sink. He splashed some cold water on his face, surprised by the sharpness of his anger. What had he ever done except be born here? He stood there for a minute, letting the water trickle down his face. The paper towel dispenser was empty, of course: the janitor, a drunk, was too lazy to fill it.

When he got to the classroom, Lorena Poot had taken her customary place in the corner, hands folded neatly on the desk, as if she'd been coming to school this whole time and he'd merely missed taking her attendance. She held her body perfectly straight, like a churchgoer. Something—the alertness of her posture, maybe—suggested that she'd wanted to return, that she'd used the watch only as an excuse. She'd forgiven him, for whatever reason. Her eyes were fierce and victorious. The other students looked at their desks, embarrassed, but Nils decided to treat this like any other day. He opened the window to let in some air. It was cool and breezy, the first cloudless day of summer. Collecting himself, he asked for a volunteer to begin the presentations, an assignment he'd invented to help them conquer their fear of interviews.

With a chivalrous leap, Edwing got up first and began his report, which he'd scrawled on the back of a postcard featuring the Golden Gate Bridge. He read the title to the class—"My Family Is So Far"—and then talked about having a wife and two sons in El Salvador, whom he was supporting with his job at Safeway. He'd owned his own distribution company in San Salvador before the *colón* plummeted. Nils, astonished, had always assumed that Edwing was single. "In conclusion," Edwing said cheerfully, "I miss my family very much." Zina, forlorn without Svetlana and somewhat confused, got up and talked about her strengths. She shouted her presentation, like a coach berating a pathetic football team. "I am team player," she said, glaring at the class. "I am independent thinker." Zhao Jun, one of the few students to fully grasp the assignment, talked about a time when she was sitting at a noodle shop in China and saw a man with no arms eating deftly with his feet. The man had had both feet propped on the table, maneuvering the chopsticks with his toes. "It was an eye opening," she said. Nils, who'd retreated to a desk in the back of the classroom, kept glancing at Lorena Poot during the presentations to judge her reaction. She seemed absorbed in the hodgepodge of stories, more interested in her fellow students than she'd ever been in him. Nils was about to let the class out early when Lorena stood up from her desk.

"I would like to make a speech," she said.

"Lorena," he said quickly, "the other students had time to prepare. I don't expect you to do a presentation."

"I am ready."

She got up before he could stop her and walked to the front of the classroom, which went unpleasantly quiet. Nils, fearing the worst, had no choice but to sit down again in the back row. Lorena stood there in front of the blackboard, surveying the silent faces with a weird smirk on her lips, as if she were about to break into a comedy routine. For a horrible second, Nils worried that she might start ridiculing him. Instead, she cleared her throat and began talking about her childhood in Yucatán, Mexico. She talked about the prosperity of her father's farm, how her mother used to teach her Mayan words before bed. She explained that her last name was Mayan, not Spanish, that it meant "to dig a deep hole in the search of water." Mayan was a language more precise than English; in fact, there were seven words for the color blue. Then she picked up the chalk and started writing the words on the board, aligning them in a straight and narrow column, just as Nils did when he was teaching new vocabulary. Lorena listed each of them, one after another, all practically the same word except for a slight variation in letters.

"This blue," she said, pointing to the first word. "This is like the ocean, the more deep part you can see in distance, where it curves. And this one is like a *loro*—a beautiful parrot in my country. And this blue, very different, like the stomach of a shark." She hesitated before explaining each of the words, briefly lifting her face to the ceiling. It occurred to Nils that she'd forgotten their real meanings. "This is the blue of my father's toenail before it falls off. Our burro would step on his foot sometimes, and it would turn the color of this. This is like your green, but we call it differently—the color of the lagoon.

And this is a fire at night, far away where you cannot hear it. And this is dark blue, almost black, like the skin of our bananas." Her face was radiant, transported. She pronounced the strange sounds carefully, cherishing them like secrets from her past. Her voice rang with confidence. Zhao Jun raised her hand from the back row, and Nils leaned toward her before realizing he couldn't answer her question. He couldn't help at all. She asked Lorena to repeat the list, and the class recited each word together, impressively, invoking the lost language as if it were their own.

Acknowledgments

I am indebted to the San Francisco Foundation, the Eastern Frontier Educational Foundation, and especially the Wallace Stegner/ John L'Heureux Fellowship at Stanford, without whose help this collection wouldn't exist.

Heartfelt thanks to the many friends and colleagues who helped me with these stories, particularly Andrew Altschul, Tom McNeely, Scott Hutchins, Mark Sundeen, Malena Watrous, and Adam Johnson. Special thanks, too, to my mentors at Stanford: John L'Heureux, Elizabeth Tallent, and Tobias Wolff. Thanks to Juan Poot, for sharing his story with me.

I owe a special debt of gratitude to Greg Martin, whose belief and investment in these stories kept me from packing it in a long time ago. Thanks so much to Dorian Karchmar, the best agent you can imagine, and to Sarah McGrath, my editor at Scribner. I'd also like to thank Tamara Straus and Michael Ray, who took a risk on an unknown writer.

Thanks to Ed Feldman, friend of a lifetime, and to Molly and Judy Breen, who supported me through the bad and reveled with me in the good.

My mother has always been there for me, unwaveringly.

Finally, I couldn't have written a word of this book without my wife, Katharine Noel, whose care, intelligence, and supernatural patience shine from every page.

About the Author

Eric Puchner teaches at Stanford University, where he was a Wallace Stegner/John L'Heureux Fellow. His short stories have appeared in the *Chicago Tribune, Zoetrope: All Story, The Missouri Review,* and *Best New American Voices 2005.* He has won a Pushcart Prize and the Joseph Henry Jackson Award for *Music Through the Floor.* He lives in San Francisco with his wife, novelist Katharine Noel.